USEFUL
PHRASES
FOR
IMMIGRANTS

USEFUL PHRASES FOR IMMIGRANTS

STORIES

May-lee Chai

BLAIR

Printed in the United States of America
Cover design by Laura Williams
Interior Design by April Leidig
Typeset in Whitman by Copperline Book Services, Inc.

Blair is an imprint of Carolina Wren Press.

*The mission of Carolina Wren Press is to seek out, nurture,
and promote literary work by new and underrepresented writers.*

This publication was made possible by Michael Bakwin's
generous establishment of the Bakwin Award for Writing by a Woman
and the continued support of Carolina Wren Press by the extended Bakwin
family. We gratefully acknowledge the ongoing support of general operations
by the Durham Arts Council's United Arts Fund and a special grant
from the North Carolina Arts Council.

Library of Congress Cataloging-in-Publication Data
Names: Chai, May-Lee, author.
Title: Useful phrases for immigrants : stories / by may-lee chai.
Description: Durham, NC : Blair, [2018]
Identifiers: LCCN 2018035244 (print) | LCCN 2018035306 (ebook) |
ISBN 9781949467093 (ebook) | ISBN 9780932112767 (alk. paper)
Classification: LCC PS3553.H2423 (ebook) |
LCC PS3553.H2423 A6 2018 (print) | DDC 813/.54—dc23
LC record available at https://lccn.loc.gov/2018035244

For my father, Winberg Chai 翟文伯

CONTENTS

USEFUL
PHRASES
FOR
IMMIGRANTS

USEFUL PHRASES FOR
IMMIGRANTS

G UILI TRIED TO glance at her watch, as she sensed time was running out, but her arms were laden with the clear, plastic containers and turning her wrist was impossible. Normally the bins were ridiculously overpriced, $24.99 each, while Guili knew they could be manufactured in Shenzhen for less than a dollar, but they were good quality, the kind with handles, and the lids stayed on. They would protect her clothes in the coming move.

Then the girl at the register barely glanced at Guili's coupon before announcing, "The promotion is over."

It was particularly infuriating because the promotion was most definitely not over. Guili had been careful to keep track of each day. Saturday she'd seen the coupon but had no time for errands. She'd had the tedious dinner with Mrs. Ma but she'd needed to curry favor with her. Mrs. Ma had been in America forever, even if she'd never bothered to properly learn English or even Mandarin; she still spoke the Cantonese dialect of her maiden village before she'd been shipped over to marry some Overseas Chinese. But Mrs. Ma's husband was an important member of the Ma Family Association. Guili had gritted her teeth and smiled and nodded and listened to the old woman's endlessly repetitive stories of her grandchildren's antics because it was important Guili's husband had good relations with the Family Associations.

Then Sunday had been cleaning and groceries and packing boxes.

Monday was the doctor appointment and afterward Guili had driven to three storage facilities. She'd had high hopes for the first— and cheapest—because her American neighbor had recommended it, but the larger units were all rented and renting two small units was no longer cheap. She'd signed the papers at the third storage place, which was far from the cheapest, but it was convenient and cleanish and the man had been kind enough to take her to look at the 10 x18 unit that would hold all the furniture and the boxes without having to resort to piling boxes on the easy chair, which over time would ruin the cushions.

Now looking back, Guili thought she'd been foolish. There was poison for rodents in the corners of each unit, the building was old. If she put the expensive armchair there, it could become infested. She'd be better off selling it. Or just throwing it away. Take the loss.

Truth was, she was tired. Her neck ached. Her cough was no better. At some point didn't the toll that work took on the body need to be taken into account?

And today, Guili had specifically planned so well. Bringing the bags and bags of receipts to be shredded, $0.99 per pound, confidentiality guaranteed, 100% SECURE the sign said in large, friendly letters. The cheerfulness of American business advertisements had been charming when she'd first arrived. None of the threats and bullying or outlandish claims she was used to. And the guilelessness of the clerks.

She hadn't been able to read between the lines then. The clerks did not try to sell her anything because their wages never went up, they were bored and demoralized, there was no point trying to bully the customer.

Guili had not expected it to be so difficult to run a business in an American recession. Movies and television shows had never shown this side. Everyone was always well-dressed and cheerful and well-fed and successful in American films, except for the villains, who were also well-dressed and well-fed and successful but so comically violent and obvious, it seemed no one had anything to fear, ever.

Why didn't people in movies complain about taxes and insurance and the cost of rent? Who needed a superhero in skin-tight circus costumes to fight aliens? The real villains were attorney's fees and lawsuits and competitors spreading bad "word of mouth."

Now the clerk was speaking again, something complicated, so Guili had to listen carefully. "The computer isn't recognizing the coupon. There's nothing I can do. It's not in the system."

"No, no, no," Guili insisted, knowing her rights. She remembered the proper phrase, took a breath, and enunciated clearly, "I would like to speak to your manager."

"The manager's out to lunch," the girl said, brazen.

"I will wait then," Guili said.

For the first time, the girl looked at her. Really looked. She was a sullen-faced young woman, with too much makeup, trying to cover her acne-ridden skin. She had on thick layers of clumpy, black mascara and her nails were elaborately colored, a different design on each finger. Guili knew this kind of girl. In China or America, they were always the same.

The girl said, "Is that coat Prada?"

Guili inhaled sharply.

In fact, it was.

"It's nice," the girl said. "I remember seeing it on the cover of *Vogue*. Anastasia Perez is my favorite actress."

"I am waiting over here," Guili said, and dragged her pile of plastic bins over to the vacant customer service counter.

GUILI, TOO, had seen this coat on the cover of *Vogue* magazine. Some thin American actress was wearing it. She hadn't cared about the actress; it was the colors of the coat that caught her eye. Plaid, green and dark blue with a fleck of red and yellow with large, old-fashioned lapels. It looked almost exactly like a coat her mother had made for Guili when she was fourteen. Her mother had given it to Guili before sending her to live with a great-aunt in Tianjin while her mother and father were being struggled against in a tedious political campaign.

Her mother had bartered for the fabric from a neighbor who had relatives overseas. That woman always had nicer things. She owed Guili's mother some kind of favor, but that wasn't why she'd given up the cloth. It was because Guili's mother had traded her grandmother's jade earrings for it.

Guili's mother was artistic and kindhearted and not good with money. These were the kinds of things that got her in trouble. But her mother knew she couldn't wear those earrings again, not ever, and if they were going to be investigated, people might come to the apartment and search through all their things and find the earrings and take them anyway. So Guili's mother had bartered them for the cloth, and then she'd stayed up all night and made the coat for Guili's trip.

No one else had cloth like that. The ration coupons that other mothers hoarded for their purchases of cloth would do no good. This fabric was special.

Under other circumstances it might have caused trouble for Guili, but in Tianjin, a city with foreign roots, her new classmates were both envious and impressed, and that had actually helped her. She seemed like the kind of girl with important parents, and people had been intimidated enough not to bully her.

Guili did not think that had been her mother's intentions actually, just good luck.

Truth be told, Guili wished her mother had kept the earrings, found a way to hide them. They could have been traded for something far more than cloth, but what could she do? Her mother was her mother.

When she saw the *Vogue* magazine with the coat just like the one her mother had made her so long ago, Guili had taken it as a sign. She'd called stores up and down the state until she'd found one that had it.

That was more than three years ago, when the business was doing well, when Guili and her husband had very high hopes for success.

AT HOME, the television was blaring in the living room. The Chinese news at 7. In China he couldn't have been bothered to watch it, but here her father-in-law couldn't bear to miss it even a single evening.

As Guili set the table, her mother-in-law was complaining. "And to think that woman was bragging about her new Lexus! I told her, you know that's a Japanese car. I wouldn't want anything those Japanese dwarves made."

Anping was passive-aggressive as ever. She knew Xiaobing would be going to Japan soon. But when Guili looked at her husband, he didn't respond. He wasn't going to speak. He wouldn't contradict his mother.

"Why do you call the Japanese 'dwarves,' Nai-nai?" Little Tiger asked.

"Because when those dwarves invaded our country—" Anping began.

"Little Tiger isn't allowed to use that kind of language," Guili said. She couldn't stand it.

"Don't call me Little Tiger anymore," Little Tiger said. "It's a baby name. I want to be Ted now," he said in English.

"*Ted?*"

"No, Ma. Ted."

"That's what I said. *Ted.*"

"No, it's not like that. Ted. Ted. Ted!" he said over and over.

Anping snorted loudly.

Guili took a deep breath. When Guili first joined this family, her in-laws still spat inside the house. After Guili had given birth, her mother-in-law could barely write the characters for the formal name Guili had chosen for him, Wei. Anping had written the character that meant strong instead of the *wei* that meant a precious kind of jade. Guili was the one who'd written the name for his birth certificate to make certain it would be correct.

She wondered sometimes how her husband could have come from this woman. Xiaobing was everything his mother was not: forward-thinking, intelligent, kind. Guili did not yet want to admit that these were not qualities businessmen in America needed so much as his mother's stubborn, ruthless pragmatism.

Anping pursed her lips as though she were sucking on a sour plum pit, weighing a new complaint. Every night it was something else. The Ranch 99 no longer carried her favorite brand of dried cuttlefish, the price of eggs was too high, the kumon in the strip mall had a waiting list.

"There's too much competition here," her mother-in-law said finally. "We're not like these rich Overseas Chinese. You should send Little Tiger to live with Xiaobing's former classmate's sister. That'll be better for him."

Little Tiger was staring at his phone. He wasn't listening, or he was pretending not to listen, or he'd lost the capacity to listen long ago and was living in blissful deafness and Guili had somehow not noticed.

The classmate's sister lived in Utah. Her husband was a short order cook. She worked as a waitress. They already owned their own house and were saving up to buy an apartment house. "Real estate, that's where the real money is," this sister said, a font of wisdom.

"Little Tiger can live with them. It'll be good for him. Xiaobing didn't live with us, and he turned out fine."

Guili hated the woman.

She closed her eyes and pressed her fingers to her temples.

Recently she had read in a magazine while waiting in the grocery store that disarming the enemy with a compliment could be a good way of getting what one wanted. What Guili wanted was quiet, one evening without her mother-in-law's voice, louder than the television, complaining about something new.

"I don't mean to criticize, Nai-nai," Guili said. "I know how you suffered in the war."

"Oh, you know, do you?" Anping shook her head. "I watched my cousin starve to death. I watched her lie down to sleep and never wake up."

Little Tiger's eyes widened.

"Ma," Xiaobing said miserably.

"What? That wasn't even suffering. That was just life. And what could I do? I was just a girl. You could lie down and die or you could stand up and try to fight."

"My wife joined the Party when she was a teenager," Guili's father-in-law piped up from his armchair. "In those days, the government could put you to death for that. But your grandmother chose to fight with Chairman Mao."

"I was a revolutionary from the beginning," Anping nodded. "We peasants had to fight every day or the landlords and the capitalists would have feasted on our bones."

"Ma," Xiaobing said. "We're all capitalists now." He winked at Little Tiger and Little Tiger smiled.

Surprised that her son had spoken up, Anping was silent for a minute. A full minute. Guili counted the seconds.

THAT NIGHT as she lay in bed, Guili listened to the wind howling outside, shaking the glass. The *Santa Ana*, the neighbors called it. A wind so treacherous it had its own name.

Her husband snored beside her, oblivious to the weather.

Before the manager at Staples had returned from his endless "lunch," Guili had had to leave to pick up Little Tiger from his after-school classes.

What she'd said to the girl at the customer service counter was "I'll take a rain check!" (She had learned this term from a book that she'd picked up at the Chinese bookstore on sale, *Useful Phrases for Immigrants*.)

Surprisingly, the girl had liked this solution. She wrote up "a ticket" for Guili and said she could return next week for her bins and she could still use the same coupon and someone else at work would have to deal with it that day.

This was a perfectly face-saving strategy and Guili would have been proud of herself if not for the fact that a week from now she'd be living in a completely different city in a different, cheaper part of the state, and the whole point of the bins was getting them *now*.

But she took the "rain check" and left.

GUILI TURNED over in their bed. She didn't want to wake Xiaobing with her restlessness, but she could find no comfortable spot on her side of the mattress. Guili worried as she did every night that they had missed their time.

Back when they'd first decided to *xia hai*, jump into the ocean and leave their government-factory jobs and strike out on their own, no obstacle seemed too harsh. They'd been willing to work hard, Xiaobing crisscrossed the country, representative of the company his classmates had formed. Guili kept the books, she saved money, economized, sacrificed; they saved and saved. They put off having a child until nearly too late, Guili was nearly forty when she gave birth. Fifteen years had flown by.

Now here they were in America finally, California, only to discover everywhere they looked, there were Chinese who'd come earlier, bought real estate when it was cheaper, started mindless businesses, and made a fortune. A woman in her mother-in-law's geriatric *taiji* group had a daughter and son-in-law with three boba shops in a strip mall on Olympic Boulevard and a son in Stanford. They owned five houses, renting all but one. With the profit from their rentals, they no longer had to work. Instead they leased their business licenses to new families, new poor immigrants willing to put in 100-hour weeks but who might never be able to pay off their debts because the economy had changed.

Meanwhile, Guili's and her husband's degrees were worthless because they weren't from one of the few Chinese universities famous in America, all their experience meaningless to the people here. She felt she'd arrived at the station only to find the train departed five minutes early, leaving her stranded on the border of her dreams, unable to make the cross.

WELL BEFORE dawn Xiaobing had to leave for his business trip to Japan. The shuttle picked him up from the house at 4:55. Guili had barely slept at all.

She sat on the edge of the bed as he dressed. She did not allow her feelings to overcome her.

She threw on her robe and made him some breakfast, heating the leftover *xifan* on the stove.

"It's not necessary. I'm not hungry," he said.

"You should eat."

But he only grabbed a banana from the kitchen counter and took it with him as his cellphone buzzed. "Shuttle's here," he said.

She let him go with a studied casualness that belied everything she felt churning in her stomach. Her performance was an act of courage, she decided. Not cowardice. No, not that at all.

Guili had read about Japanese businessmen. She imagined her husband drinking half the night and becoming very ill. She imagined him sick, his face leaden, retching in a modern, Japanese toilet, the kind with a seat warmer, three nozzles for wiping the shit from the ass so one never had to so much as touch a piece of toilet paper ever. *World Journal* was filled with such stories. And the men's trip to brothels, to bath houses with Japanese prostitutes. She knew from how the Japanese had operated in China how they must do business at home. But the bills were piling up. It would be important for her husband to succeed on this trip.

At breakfast, Guili looked at her husband's empty space at the table.

Her heart beat fast in her chest.

The TV was blaring, but this time with the *Today* show, her mother-in-law's favorite, and the sound of Americans laughing circled in her ears.

The kitchen table, the wind against the windows, the faces of her in-laws, her father-in-law's doughy jowls, her mother-in-law's knitted brows. Guili forced her eyes wide open, she refused to blink, but her chest hurt. The world was melting, the edges and the corners bending and running together.

She took a shallow breath, and it hurt her lungs.

Her in-laws gazed at the television, her son stared at his phone. Guili felt completely alone.

All at once the tears came burning to her eyes. Guili picked up her rice bowl from the table, her first instinct to keep her hands busy. She meant to carry it into the kitchen, something to do, something to hide the fact that she was going to cry. But as she felt the bowl in her hands, the glass cool and smooth against her skin, she felt a new urge. Facing her family, Guili raised the bowl above her head then dashed it against the floor.

The glass broke into a thousand shards.

Her father-in-law jumped in his chair. "What? What happened?"

"Clumsy," Guili said out loud, as though it had been an accident. Secretly she felt a little shiver of delight.

All eyes were on her. They were looking at her for the first time in a very long while.

Guili thought about all she could say while she had their attention. But her mother-in-law spoke first.

"It's nothing. She's just on edge. Because of the doctor," Anping whispered loudly.

"What?"

But Anping didn't answer. She went into the kitchen and returned with the dustpan.

Her father-in-law turned back to the television, her son to his phone. The moment was lost.

"Nai-nai, let me get that," Guili said at last.

"No, no, no. Don't bother. You're sick. You should rest."

"What are you talking about?"

Guili's mother-in-law began wiping the floor in exaggerated circles with a napkin, sighing like a martyr. "I wasn't going to tell you yet. The doctor called. She left a message. Call her back. So I did."

"You called my doctor?"

"Her assistant. She said your test is positive."

"She did not. You can't say these things over the phone." (There was an entire chapter in the phrase book called "Know Your Rights" with sections on Store Clerks, School Teachers, Police, Landlords, Doctors. Guili could hear the clear voice of the instructor from the accompanying CD: *Repeat after me. I know my rights. You cannot do this. I know my rights.*)

Her mother-in-law was nonchalant. "She mistook me for you. We have the same voice to these Americans. She said you need to make an appointment to come to their office." Anping stood up and stretched her back. "I don't want to cause trouble. I don't want to argue with you. You should conserve your strength. I didn't want to say anything while Xiaobing was here. No point worrying him."

Guili's heart beat like a drum in her ears.

Guili turned her back on her mother-in-law and the blaring television and she marched past the battalion of boxes that lined the hall and marched up the stairs to her bedroom and shut the door, not even slamming it. She pushed a tower of three packing boxes against it. And then she opened her closet, all the clothes yet unpacked; she'd wanted to wait till the last possible minute to prevent wrinkling, which seemed foolish now, stupid even, laughable. She slipped her arms around her coat, while it was still on the hanger. She put her hand in the pocket. She stroked the sleeve. The Italian fabric was smooth to the touch. Soft.

Guili remembered the morning that her mother had given her the coat.

Her father was startled when he saw it. Then he was furious. He'd marched across their apartment to the wooden box where her mother kept their ration coupons and he'd dumped the small slips of paper for flour and rice and cooking oil onto the table top. "What have you done?"

And her mother had laughed, inexplicably, and said, "What are a few coupons worth compared to our daughter?"

And in his rage, her father had raised his hand as though he meant to slap her mother.

Whether for using up the coupons or for laughing at him or for all the million other things in his life he could not control, it was hard to tell.

"Don't hit my mother!" Guili had shouted, but her mother grabbed her by the arms and pulled her out the door, saying, "Hush, the neighbors."

Guili's father then smashed the rice bowls, one after the other. "Foolish!" he shouted, a bowl shattering against the floor. *Ben dan!* Stupid egg!

Guili could hear the glass breaking through the closed door as she and her mother walked down the stairs of the apartment building together. In his rage, her father seemed to forget it was Guili's last morning at home.

On the walk to the long-distance bus station, the early morning light clean and pure against the sidewalk, her mother had explained that she'd hidden all their ration coupons for cloth in advance. In order to keep him from suspecting that she'd traded the earrings. "Your father would not understand," she said.

On an ordinary day, Guili might have said, "He's a counter-revolutionary! All he thinks are feudal thoughts!" her usual teenage sullenness, but this morning Guili had been too shocked to reply.

Real jade, just for some cloth. And the wool wasn't heavy. The coat in fact was not quite warm enough even on this spring morning.

But it was too late, and her mother was so happy, her cheeks flushed red in the wind. She looked youthful and pleased. "Remember, Guili," she whispered, "I wanted you to have something beautiful." Then she'd slipped her arm through Guili's and the two of them had walked to the bus station together like this, arm in arm like schoolgirls with no cares in the world despite the fact that everything familiar and safe in their world was ending.

This feeling of hopeless hope or suspended despair or temporary consolation amidst unknowingness, Guili thought, was the phrase missing from her book. How useful it would have been to name this feeling exactly in this new and perilous land.

She slipped her arms into the coat sleeves; the expensive cloth— silk, cotton, and 3 percent cashmere—felt like an embrace, like a promise, like good luck. She'd known the love of her mother, who was willing to sacrifice her most treasured possession just to make Guili a coat. That love felt like the Prada. It gave Guili confidence.

And she at long last understood her father's rage. For the unjust nature of life.

In an hour or so, Guili knew that she would call the doctor and find out the news herself, what the test results meant, what kind of suffering was in store for her and how expensive it would be. And she would use this answer, whatever it was, as an excuse to send her in-laws back to Henan. Her husband was gone, busy; he wouldn't be able to fly back and intervene. Later she would claim that she'd acted out of consideration for Anping, how Guili hadn't wanted to burden the old woman who, after all, already had her aged husband to look after. How would it look if Guili had allowed her mother-in-law to take care of her, too? Xiaobing would not be able to fault her logic.

Guili imagined the old woman's surprise. Outfoxed in the last move.

And then it occurred to her, the exact useful word she needed. Guili could hear it enunciated in her ear in the soft flat voice of the woman who read all the English phrases on the CD. *Checkmate.*

FISH BOY

H EY, KID, YOU just gonna sit there?" The Boss was standing
in front of Xiao Yu. Xiao Yu recognized the man's polished
leather shoes, the cuffs of his expensive pants, his complicated watch, the clean white cuffs of his shirt. Out of politeness
he'd never stared the man in the face. Now Xiao Yu stood up and
stared at the man's shoes.

"No, Uncle," he said politely as his grandfather had instructed
him to say. "I can work, too."

"Work?" The Boss laughed. The men in the kitchen laughed.
"The squirt wants to work, did you hear that?" The Boss put his
hand on top of Xiao Yu's head. He could feel the sweat of the man's
palms dripping through his hair to his scalp. "And what can you
do, Squirt?"

"I can scale fish. I know how to kill chickens. I can—"

"Whoa, whoa, listen to this! The squirt really does want to
work!" The Boss pulled a pack of cigarettes out of the pocket of his
crisp white shirt and tapped one out for himself. "Fine, fine, glad
to hear you can be useful. Country kids, much better than a city
brat," the Boss said. "A kid who's willing to work." He tapped one
of the men with the cleavers between the shoulder blades. "You!
Show the kid how it works with the fish. Kid wants to scale fish,
let him."

Xiao Yu's heart jumped inside his ribcage. To earn real money! The Boss headed toward the door. He turned, jabbing his cigarette in the air at Xiao Yu's nose. "Show me what you're worth, kid, and maybe I'll hire you, too." Then he opened the door—the sound of a woman singing a Hong Kong pop song momentarily flooded the kitchen along with a thousand dots of colored light from the mirrored disco balls—then the Boss was gone and the door swung shut.

"Fuck his mother! What am I supposed to do? Babysit?" The man with the cleaver spat on the kitchen floor.

"I know how to scale—"

"Yeah, yeah, yeah. You know everything. I heard you. But this is the city. Things are different here." The man sighed. "Come with me."

He led Xiao Yu to a little room just to the side of the kitchen where the walls were lined with fish tanks. Just then one of the waitresses dressed in a shiny red qipao slit to her thigh hurried in. "Give me a grouper, quick! Make it a big one."

The man grabbed a net and fished a grouper out of one of the tanks and slipped it quickly into a yellow plastic box, where it flipped and flopped, gasping for breath.

"That good enough, Little Sister?"

"Watch your mouth. I'm not your sister," she said, and picked up the box and took it outside.

"All right, kid, now do you remember what that fish looked like?"

"Yes. It's a gray fish with dark spots—"

"Yeah, yeah. I mean, the size? You think you could find its twin?"

"All groupers look like that."

"Fuck. This kid is straight off the farm." The man shook his head, but he took Xiao Yu by the shoulder and led him down the line of tanks, past crabs and lobsters, past lively colored fish that shone like gemstones, to a row of tanks packed so full of fish they could barely move. Many were ill, gray-white fungus growing from their gills, floating listlessly on their sides, their fins beating the dingy water futilely. "Find the grouper in this tank that looks exactly like the one we put in the box, and be quick."

"But none of these fish look like that one. These fish are sick—"

"They're okay, they're going to die soon anyway. Consider it a blessing to kill them. Do you believe in the Buddha's teachings?"

"The Buddha?"

The man shook his head. "Never mind. Just find the fish. Hurry up."

Xiao Yu scanned the filthy tank. The sides were covered with algae, even the light bulb under the lid was covered with a greenish growth. "That one's the same size."

"Get it then." The man handed a net hanging from a nail on the wall to Xiao Yu.

Xiao Yu lifted the lid gingerly and peered into the densely packed tank. He stuck the net in, trying not to accidentally scoop up the wrong fish, but it proved difficult to net the large grouper that was floating on its side slowly up and down toward the back of the tank. Other fish kept bumping it away or swam into the net. Xiao Yu had never seen such sick fish. Finally, he dropped the net onto the floor and rolled up the sleeve of his good sweater, the one his grandfather had insisted he wear to his First Week of Work, and stuck his right hand into the brine. He was able to grab the sick grouper by the gills and pull it up.

"Hey, that's a useful trick." The man nodded approvingly. "Here, put it in this bag." The man grabbed a plastic bag from a pile on the shelf under the tank and held it open so Xiao Yu could slip the grouper inside. It barely flopped at all. The only sign that it hadn't died yet was the way the plastic was sucked into the fish's gills as it tried to breathe, slowly suffocating in the dry air.

Suddenly the waitress reappeared and set the yellow plastic box on the ground next to the tank of healthy fish. "They want it steamed with garlic, ginger, and chives. No hot sauce this time." She ran out again.

The man lifted the box and quickly dumped the lively grouper back into the clean tank, where it flipped once, twice, and then began to swim rapidly back and forth, as though it thought it might be able to swim away and escape.

"You heard her. Show me how you kill a fish now, clean it, and then I'll show you which cook to give it to."

"Won't the customers get angry?"

"They'll be too drunk by the time they get to the fish course to even notice." Then the man winked at Xiao Yu in a way that made him feel older, a part of things. Clever like these men, not like city kids who didn't know how to work, like the Boss had said. Not like a kid at all really. And Xiao Yu squared his shoulders and stood a little taller.

AFTER HE'D been cleaning fish for four hours, Xiao Yu's shoulders ached from hunching over the bucket where he was told to dump the scales and the guts. The smoke from the woks and the men's cigarettes made his throat burn. Fatigued, the men had stopped yelling jokes and obscenities at each other. It was as if the night were flipping on its belly, like the fish in the filthy tank. Trapped amongst the other men, Xiao Yu felt the kitchen growing smaller, closing in on him, too. He imagined stretching out on his bunkbed in the dormitory. It would feel good to be able to stretch at all.

"Hey, kid, time to empty the buckets. We've got to get rid of this smell. Smells like a toilet in here. From now on, don't wait so long. Throw the guts out back in the trash before we've got piles building up. This isn't some farm."

Xiao Yu bristled at the man's insult, his cheeks burning hot, hot. He wanted to take his fish knife and hook the man who'd insulted him.

But he thought about his grandfather and the money they'd be making, and maybe they'd be able to hire a real lawyer for his father—he wasn't supposed to have heard about that, but he'd overheard his grandparents talking when they thought he was asleep on the train. If they could hire a city lawyer, his father would be all right. They just needed more money.

Xiao Yu would show these men then. He'd expose their corrupt restaurant to the police. With their rotten food and their dirty tricks. He'd show them a country boy wasn't so stupid after all.

But for now he picked up four of the buckets of guts, two in each hand, and carried them to the back door. He wasn't afraid to work. He'd make his family proud.

The night air was cool against Xiao Yu's flushed cheeks. When they'd first arrived in Zhengzhou, he'd found the air gritty, strange, with a smell so different from the village air that he had pretended in his head that he was a taikonaut, the first Chinese on the moon, and he was walking in a heavy white suit with a fishbowl helmet over his head. The air he was forced to breathe, recycled and coming from tanks on his back, smelled like Zhengzhou's air. Like air that had already been breathed in and exhaled by nine million people. But after four hours in the smoky kitchen squatting over the buckets of fish guts, he found the night air no longer smelled so bad. It wasn't country air, but it wasn't kitchen air either.

He put the buckets down for a second and allowed his weary lungs to breathe deeply before he set off for the dumpsters. He closed his eyes, listening to the distant sounds of traffic, horns honking, voices of invisible people arguing and laughing, a bus rumbling by on the street beyond the alleyway. Then it was time to get back to work.

Xiao Yu was gingerly pouring the first bucket's bloody contents into the dumpster in the dark alley behind the restaurant when a *ping!* like the shot from an air rifle ricocheted off the dumpster's metal side. He turned around immediately. There was a group of boys on bicycles, fancy bikes, the kind he'd seen on TV, the kind you could do tricks with: wide tires, low handlebars, bright colors. City bikes.

"Hey, Little Rabbit, what's up?"

Xiao Yu eyed the four boys arrayed between him and the door of the restaurant. They were older, high school students, he guessed. And there were four of them.

He didn't want to speak, afraid his accent would give him away.

"What's the matter? You a mute?"

The tallest boy approached. The others circled closer. Xiao Yu put the bucket down and wiped his slick hands on the sides of his pants, even though they were his best pants and he wasn't supposed to get them dirty. He'd been very careful in the kitchen actually, leaning far over the buckets so the guts wouldn't splatter. Finally, one of the cooks had given him an apron and he'd spread it carefully over his pants, purchased by his father from the city just for this trip so that he'd blend in with the other city kids. He'd been proud. Proud to have new clothes, even if they'd been purchased to make it easier to hide, so police wouldn't spot them on the streets, the way they imagined, and send them back to the village. They hadn't realized how little anyone in the city would care about their appearance. "You look like a young man now," his grandfather had said proudly, seeing Xiao Yu in his new clothes. "No one will know you haven't grown up your whole life in a city." All these thoughts circled through Xiao Yu's mind as he eyed the boys.

"What're you doing here?" A boy with a round face and flat nose pointed his chin at Xiao Yu. He had extremely small eyes, making his face seem more pig-like than a normal human's. The tall boy stood back now. Xiao Yu figured he was the leader. The other two boys were thinner, acne dotting their cheeks. As they approached, Xiao Yu could see they chewed their lips. They were cowards. They would be the ones he should attack first if it came to that. It was going to come to that. He felt the hair on his neck rise. He could feel the sweat pouring from his armpits.

"This is our alley. What are *you* doing here, Little Rabbit?"

"I work for the restaurant. The boss told me to—"

The boys charged. They were faster than he thought. The two skinny ones grabbed him from behind, twisting his arms up into the air behind his back; the pig-eyed boy punched him in the stomach.

Xiao Yu thought he might throw up. The alley turned completely black.

Now the boys were kicking him. He couldn't even call out. The nausea was overwhelming. He wretched. He hadn't eaten all night, there was nothing to throw up, but he wretched again.

The tall boy came over and he felt hands going through the pockets of his pants. "No money. This *tu baozi* is as poor as he looks." He felt the boy's spit land on his face.

Then the boys were kicking him again, and he curled into a ball. "Hey, hey, watch this! Watch me!" It was Pig Eyes's voice.

Suddenly Xiao Yu felt wet slimy entrails raining down upon his head.

Laughter.

The blood made him want to wretch again. But something about the cold fish guts revived him. His vision was returning.

The city boys were bent over laughing. They were turning away, going to their bicycles.

Xiao Yu felt along the ground searching for a rock. He had good aim. He could make a stone skip thirteen times atop a fish pond. He wouldn't miss, even now. But he could find no rocks.

The boys were retreating.

Then Xiao Yu's fingers felt the beer bottle. It was broken, empty, rolled beneath the dumpster. He gripped it tightly.

He staggered to his feet, and with the adrenaline and anger just enough to make him dangerous, he found he could run. He ran toward the city boys and lobbed the bottle as hard as he could at the back of the tall boy's head. It struck, shattering against the boy's skull.

The tall boy dropped his bicycle and clutched his head with both hands.

"That mother fuck!" The pig-eyed boy turned toward Xiao Yu.

"Beat his balls off!" the tall boy gasped. Blood, black in the dim light, gushed from between his fingers.

"Fuck your mother, Rabbit Boy!" The skinny boys rushed him.

Xiao Yu retreated to the dumpster, and one of the boys slipped on the spilled fish guts. Xiao Yu managed to punch the other skinny boy in the face, but then Pig Eyes grabbed him tightly, wrapped his arms around his chest, squeezing so that Xiao Yu couldn't breathe. He thought his back would break.

He shouted now. He howled.

"I'll fuck your mother and your grandmother!" Pig Eyes slammed Xiao Yu against the dumpster.

Xiao Yu's head struck the metal with a loud thunk.

"Cut his face." The tall boy approached, his left hand still holding the back of his head. In his right hand he held a piece of broken glass. "Hold him still and I'll cut the fucking eyes out of this bumpkin's head."

Xiao Yu felt the boys' hands around his arms and legs, around his neck, as he tried to squirm free, but Pig Eyes was big. He leaned his weight into Xiao Yu, setting a knee on his chest.

Then a triangle of light flooded from the open kitchen door.

"Hey, you little bastards, get the hell away from here!"

One of the cooks had come out to see what was taking Xiao Yu so long. He was carrying a cleaver. The light behind him, he appeared in silhouette, as black as the sky.

"My father will put you in jail. Do you know who I am?" the tall boy shouted back.

"You're going to be tonight's main course if you don't get your junior-high ass off the Boss's property! Do you know who owns this restaurant?"

"My father will have this restaurant closed down! My father will have all of you thrown back to the countryside where you belong! My father—"

"Your father's going to bury his son in a paper bag."

The cook turned back and shouted something into the restaurant. A burly man with a bald head and a large tattoo on the side of his neck, spiraling up the side of his cheek, appeared.

"You have no idea who you're talking to. You're just workers." The tall boy tried to laugh, but even to Xiao Yu's ringing ears, his voice sounded less confident.

The burly man didn't stop to talk, he approached the boys rapidly. They backed away from Xiao Yu, standing away from the tall boy, too. Xiao Yu watched the world from the asphalt, through his one eye that wasn't swollen shut yet.

The burly man went right up to the tall boy and pulled out something shiny. Xiao Yu thought it might be a knife. He pointed it at the boy's face.

"You wouldn't dare. My father will—"

The man pointed the shiny object at the brick wall beside the restaurant and fired his gun. It was louder than any gun Xiao Yu had ever heard. In the countryside, when men hunted with their air rifles and ancient weapons, the sound of gunfire was absorbed by the huge open sky, not like the sky here, which was small and distant, trapped between buildings. Lights turned on from the windows at the tops of several buildings. But more lights went out.

The man pointed the gun at the tall boy's face and pulled the trigger. Even Xiao Yu could hear the click. Unmistakable. But there was no bullet. The man cocked the gun once more.

The man said, "Do you think I have another bullet or not, little shit?"

The boys took off running. They ran to their bikes, jumped on them, and rode off into the night.

The burly man re-entered the restaurant. Now two of the cooks rushed to his side. Xiao Yu recognized them from the smell of the garlic and cigarette smoke on their skin. His vision wasn't so good anymore. The world was a blur of light and shadow and more shadow.

"Look what those little hoodlums did to the fish boy," he heard one say.

"He's fresh from the countryside, this one. Has no idea how the city operates."

"Hard worker though."

"All right, help me pick him up."

Xiao Yu felt the men grab him under his arms and drag him

toward the light coming from the open kitchen door. He recognized the smell of smoke billowing into the night air.

The two men stopped to inspect him. "He doesn't look that bad. He's just beat up a bit. Still got all his parts."

"Hey, you're lucky," one of the men shouted into his ear.

"My shoes. They took my shoes."

"What? What was that?"

"Don't try to talk, kid. Not tonight. Give it a few days."

"My good shoes," Xiao Yu tried again, but the men couldn't understand him.

That night he didn't have to gut any more fish. The Boss came in briefly; he could tell from the man's voice and the way the kitchen grew quiet when he entered. Someone gave Xiao Yu a glass of hot water and some pills to take. Then one of the cooks helped him to wash in the kitchen staff's toilet. It was a filthy room, the toilet was stopped up, and the whole room smelled of urine. Xiao Yu barely moved as the young cook washed Xiao Yu's face, splashing water from the sink on him, over and over. The water was cold. It hurt and it didn't hurt. Everything hurt and nothing hurt. His body was throbbing, beating along with his heart. He was floating. He was watching this shadow self covered in blood and fish guts slumped against the wall in his underwear, this boy being doused with water from the rusty pipes.

Xiao Yu thought of how clean his grandmother had kept their indoor toilet back home. She would never let any room in their house become this filthy. They lived like civilized people. Xiao Yu remembered his father supervising as the men had put in the pipes, then the sit-down toilet, even the shower and the water heater so they could have both hot and cold water inside their home. Their house was clean. He would never walk into anyone's home with his shoes on. Here, people wore their shoes indoors all the time. In the dormitory, he'd seen men sleeping in their shoes even.

Xiao Yu had never imagined that city people would be so unclean.

"HURRY UP, kid. There's blood everywhere. Don't just sit on your ass all night."

Xiao Yu jumped up from his stool beside the bucket over which he gutted the fish and grabbed the mop from the storeroom beside the smelly, bubbling, overpacked fish tanks. Seven months in the city and the filth no longer fazed him at work or in the streets or in the dormitory.

Xiao Yu grabbed the metal bucket, filled it with water from the concrete sink there, and mopped up the entrails spilling onto the kitchen floor. Chicken guts, duck guts, goose guts, fish guts, snake guts, even lizard guts. (Lizard was the week's special. Xiao Yu had never imagined the prices city people would pay to eat food a farmer would eat only in times of great famine. The cooks laughed about it and then shrugged.)

Life in the restaurant had taken on a kind of sameness: filth and shouting, the same jokes, the same insults. The Boss barked orders at the cooks, the busboys, even a couple of the waitresses in their shiny, too-tight qipaos. The Boss's cigarette butt dangled perilously over a dish of *ma po doufu* he inspected, until, satisfied with his power, he pulled his pants up a bit—they tended to slip down beneath his bulging gut, *like a pregnant woman's,* Xiao Yu thought—and rushed back out into the dining room to banter obsequiously with the drunken customers.

"*Ta ma de,*" one of the cooks swore, tossing a heavy iron wok full of shrimp. The flames leaped up, following the oily wok, licking its round bottom. Nonchalantly, the cook tossed in a dash of spiced oil, steam emerging in a cloud, and set the wok back down over the possessive fire. The room soon filled with the smell of hot Sichuan peppers.

"Whad'ya do that for?" Another cook coughed and spat on the floor. "Hey, kid, open the back door. We'll all suffocate in here. That rabbit's daughter is trying to kill us." He coughed some more.

"Ha! This is how you make Sichuan shrimp. You people can't handle a little spice."

Xiao Yu set the mop in the concrete sink then carried the bucket of bloody water in one hand, the bucket of miscellaneous entrails in the other. He headed toward the back door, stopping only once to set the heavy buckets down for a moment, wipe his hands on his cotton pants, and slip a knife from the counter into his pocket, a pack of cigarettes up his right sleeve.

He left the door propped open with a stone, just wide enough to let in fresh air—and so that he could hear the cooks arguing—but not so wide that they could see him make his way through the alley to the dumpster behind the restaurant.

Four boys were waiting for him.

"What took you so long? It's cold out here."

"I could have taken a shit if I'd known you were gonna be so late tonight."

"What's stopping you now? Wanna shit, go shit," Xiao Yu shot back. Then he pulled out the knife and the pack of cigarettes.

"That's nothing," one of the older boys sneered. "Tiny knife like that."

"Oh yeah?" Xiao Yu scratched the tip across the metal of the dumpster. It left an impressive scar.

"Chef's knife. Nothing sharper."

"Shit! How'd you get that?" one of the boys gasped.

"Never mind. What have you got?"

One of the boys pulled out a crumpled pack of Panda brand cigarettes and a whistle. The other boys including Xiao Yu groaned. "That's nothing. Send that home to your grandma for Tomb Sweeping Day. She can leave it on the graves she sweeps."

"What about you?"

The others brought out knives, a rusted cleaver, a set of tools— screwdrivers with different size heads and a few hammers, and a bottle of clear white rice wine.

"That's as small as your penis!" one of the boys sneered.

"What are you looking at his penis for?"

The boys laughed. The angry boy threatened to kick the mouthy one. They got over it.

"Hurry up. I can't stay out here forever."

"I'll trade you my knife for the *bai jiu*." Xiao Yu nodded at the wine.

"No way. That's genuine Maotai. Know how much that costs?"

"Let's drink it," someone suggested.

"Don't be stupid. I could sell this for money."

"My knife and the cigarettes. They're foreign. American brand. Smoother than Chinese. I've smoked them."

"They wouldn't give you one."

"Sure did."

"Okay." The boy handed the expensive, tiny bottle of liquor to Xiao Yu. He put it into his pants pocket. Then thinking better, tucked it into the hidden pocket his grandmother had sewn into the interior of his t-shirt, just in case there was some emergency and a hidden pocket might come in handy. At the time, Xiao Yu had had no idea what she was thinking. Now he appreciated her guile.

Before anyone could object or try to negotiate a better trade, Xiao Yu dumped his buckets into the dumpster and ran back toward the kitchen, leaving the other boys, all restaurant workers from the neighborhood, to bargain over the remaining loot.

THE NEXT morning, Xiao Yu woke early as usual. His grandfather was snoring, exhausted from his night job. He slept like the dead, unmoving, his body stretched out straight and stiff across his bunk-bed, dressed in his clothes. He'd been too tired to remove them after he got back to the dormitory. As usual. If not for the potent snorts and hoots that emerged from his nose, his grandfather could truly have been mistaken for dead, Xiao Yu thought. It was a good thing the other men sleeping here were just as exhausted or they might have complained. But in the dormitory they were all migrants, none of them with a legal work permit; no one complained about noise.

Xiao Yu zipped his jacket and grabbed his shoes from under the bed, then ran out of the dormitory quietly. He didn't stop running even as he slipped his feet into his sneakers, sprinting down the hallway that led to the toilets. The light was dim from the tiny windows. Not yet dawn but soon. The night-shift workers had come to bed at four. The day-shift workers would begin rising at five. He had the hallway to himself, the air reverberating around him with snores.

The window opposite the toilets didn't close properly. The men kept jacking it open, to mitigate the smell. It was the only window in the entire dormitory that wasn't sealed and locked. Xiao Yu hiked it up easily, wincing at its squeak, but no one came from the factory or the toilet or the dormitory. He squeezed through the opening and dropped to the ground some six, seven feet below. The window was unsteady. It would squeak its way down soon enough, as Xiao Yu had discovered. Now he ran, as fast he could, but quiet-quiet, too, so as not to wake the guard dogs in the cages on the sides of the courtyard where the morning shift workers were required to gather for morning exercises or pep talks or simply to stand while being shouted at by the bosses through loudspeakers. Sometimes if a worker tried to leave his shift early, they'd stick him in the dog cages or make him kneel on the concrete in the sun as punishment, the dogs barking behind him. The bosses threatened to release the dogs if the man didn't obey. The men always obeyed. Xiao Yu kept scraps from the restaurant in his pockets. If the dogs woke, he threw them the meat through the bars of their iron cages. They knew him by now. They wouldn't bark long. The dogs were like men. They only worked because they were hungry.

Xiao Yu made it to the end of the courtyard. The sky was lightening. Dawn was coming. Soon the drunk who sat in the gatehouse checking the identification cards of everyone who entered or left the factory compound would wake. Then there'd be problems. But now as Xiao Yu crept to the gatehouse and peered in its window he could see the man slumped over his desk, snoring into the crook of his arm. Xiao Yu slipped past him to the front gate, which was easier to climb over than the stone walls with strands of barbed wire and broken glass embedded in the cement on top. Not that he hadn't learned to scale those walls, but he preferred not to. Didn't want to risk a tear in his city jeans, the pair he'd bought with his own money. Now he climbed the metal bars of the front gate and hauled himself to the top where the bars turned to sharp spikes. He balanced on the horizontal metal beam, careful to fit his feet between the spikes. This was the tricky part. If he lost his balance, he'd fall twelve feet to the concrete below. Or worse, if he slipped just a bit, he'd fall upon a spike. But Xiao Yu didn't slip. He never even worried that he would. It was too exciting to escape the dark, snore-filled, fart-filled, old-man-smell-filled dormitory and roam the city streets and alleys. He was almost fourteen. There was nothing he felt he couldn't do.

Xiao Yu ran through the streets. There was already traffic. There was always traffic in the city. People working, getting off work, going to work, stumbling from bars, stumbling into bars, lurching about the sidewalks, strolling with friends, running from enemies; sidewalk vendors, small shop owners, big club owners, farmers in tattered clothes selling fruit from baskets, beggars, pickpockets, gamblers, hookers, foreigners, buses, trucks, taxis, cars, bicycles. He met up with his new city friends in the alley behind the department store with the giant billboard of some Korean movie star smiling in front. The boys were already well into their game. A pile of crumpled bills, bartered weapons—knives, cleavers, rusted pointed things—foreign candy, favorite snacks, and a watch lay in the middle of the circle of boys as they tossed their cards down, grabbed up others.

Then the boys compared hands, and after much groaning, one boy swept up the pile into his knapsack.

Another boy began dealing a new round. He flipped the cards expertly. Big Ears's skill was a thing of beauty. His hands, normally thick and stubby-fingered, dirt under his nails, became as graceful as a wushu artist's, as fast as Jet Li when he shot the cards through the air.

"Are you in?" one of the boys asked without looking up. He rearranged his cards.

Xiao Yu threw down a few of the bills he was paid by the boss for gutting fish and other animals all night.

"Of course I'm in. Prepare to lose."

"Ha! You don't have the money. You'll fold before we get to the third round."

They laughed, they swore, they shared some stolen cigarettes and a can of Coca-Cola mixed with a bottle of cheap *bai jiu.* Xiao Yu was never more aware of how useless his schooling had been, all those years memorizing all those worthless characters, reading those old boring essays, when the real world was out here, on the street, made up of money and fast hands, faster feet. This life was an education. His old life was like a long dream, one only his grandfather still believed in. The dream of school and his father returning from prison and the family together in the village. If Xiao Yu thought of such things at all, it seemed to him his entire family was living in a coma. Only he was awake.

When Xiao Yu returned in the afternoon, after shoplifting with his friends, extorting money from younger kids on their way to and from school, and fighting with rival gangs, he never told his grandfather about his real life, about the real world that Xiao Yu had discovered and now inhabited and intended to learn how to survive in. No, how to *thrive* in. He was a good student after all. He'd just been studying the wrong material.

When he returned to the dormitory, brazenly walking through the front gate this time, bribing the afternoon gatekeeper with some of his day's earnings, Xiao Yu told his grandfather that he'd been to school. It was only a half day because he was a migrant in the city, no residence permit, so he had to go to a charity school run by some do-gooders, but at least some schooling was better than none. And his grandfather smiled, the folds around his eyes deepening, the happiness on his face evident. He patted Xiao Yu on the head. "Study hard. Be sure to study hard for your father. He's worked all these years just for you." And Xiao Yu nodded and pretended to be both astonished and thrilled by the crumpled ten-yuan note his grandfather slipped into his hand with a wink. "Be sure to buy yourself a snack after school tomorrow. Something the city kids like. You might as well get used to this lifestyle. Learn what it's like. No point acting like an old man before your time."

Xiao Yu nodded. "Thank you, Ye-ye," he said.

"You're my grandson," Ye-ye replied. "I want you to have the best. Remember you're just as good as these spoiled city kids. Better. You know how to work harder." Then he quoted the proverb about fish and birds: a fish is bound only by the sea, a bird by the sky. It was supposed to mean Xiao Yu could go far in the world if he put his mind to it.

Xiao Yu hung his head, stared at his sneakers, feigning modesty. But truly he thought his grandfather was correct. This was the one point where they indeed saw eye to eye. Xiao Yu knew that he was as good as these city boys, better even, because he saw more clearly than they. They were fish in a bowl; only he had leapt into the sea.

GHOST FESTIVALS

U NCLE LINCOLN CALLED to ask me if I'd heard the news. It was all over the Internet. "The Pope has come out in favor of gay marriage! He said it in a press conference in Rome. It's amazing, Lu-ying," he said. "I never thought I'd live to see this day."

I didn't have the heart to tell him it was a hoax. The same as the reports that Pope Francis had said Hell was a literary device. My friends had been "liking" it all day on Facebook, until someone thought to check Snopes. But on the other hand, who knew? Maybe this pope really did think these things and it was only the public airing that was false.

"I thought of your mother today," Uncle Lincoln said.

"Because of the pope?"

"No, because it's your parents' anniversary."

Oh, shit, I thought. I'd completely forgotten. "Did you call my dad?"

"I left a message. He didn't answer."

"He'll be happy you remembered," I said. I glanced at the clock on the wall. Still time before it was midnight in New Jersey. I could call right after Lincoln hung up.

"Of course!" he said, his voice offended. "I never forget."

"I know, I'm sorry," I said.

"I always light a candle for your mother on my shrine. I've got my own ancestor altar set up, with pictures of Ba and Ma, and of course your mother."

"Did you put it up for Qing Ming?"

"No, Qing Ming is next month," Uncle Lincoln explained patiently. "I keep the candle up year round."

I couldn't keep track of when Chinese New Year fell, much less the festivals for the dead. It wasn't just that the lunar calendar threw me, but the fact that Chinese traditionally celebrated the dead more than the living. Birthdays didn't count, everyone used to add a year on the first day of Spring Festival (a.k.a. Chinese New Year), but memorial days were essential. There was the forty-ninth day after death when the gates of the underworld opened and the newly departed could finally go to the other side, the official Ghost Day when we were supposed to burn incense money and set out plates of fruit for hungry ghosts wandering in between reincarnations, anniversaries of deaths of grandparents and ancestors I'd never met, Qing Ming for sweeping the tombs (or changing the flowers in front of my paternal grandparents' mausoleum). When I was younger, I'd never understood why it was important to memorialize death days more than birthdays.

But what really made me marvel was thinking that Uncle Lincoln still carried a candle for my mother. She'd dated him first before she met my father. Not that they'd ever been serious, but I think she represented something glamorous to Lincoln, some fantasy version of his life, the path not taken, all that. They used to like to dress up and go to parties in Manhattan, Broadway plays, recitals by famous musicians. "I must have known," Mom would later say of their time together. "He had a roommate and the roommate always acted so jealous whenever I came over, but we never talked about such things in those days."

I don't know if he ever knew about her taking part in the letter campaign to get *Soap* taken off the air because Billy Crystal played a gay man trying to win custody of his child. It was 1977, before Lincoln came out, and the church had condemned the show. My mother, dutiful Catholic, wrote her letters without ever watching an episode. I saw them in the typewriter that summer.

I watched an episode secretly after I eavesdropped on her conversation with Sister Kevin. I checked the *TV Guide*, planned a distraction with the dogs, and turned to the channel while Mom was busy. All I remember was how boring it was. All these grown-ups talking talking talking.

The Hardy Boys/Nancy Drew Mysteries had started the same year. It was all I could talk about. I collected the cover profiles of Pamela Sue Martin from *People* and *Tiger Beat*; I had the lunch box, the t-shirts, the matching notebooks and folders. Mom was worried and had complained to Sister Kevin about me: "I'm afraid Lu-ying loves that TV show more than God." Sister Kevin, bless her, had reassured Mom that it was just a phase, "Every girl loves Nancy Drew." I loved Sister then, too.

I REMEMBER that summer well. I was going to start junior high, I was going to turn twelve. My father was busy teaching summer school and worrying about money; my mother was overseeing the construction on our house and worrying about money. There were strange men coming in and out, fixing the carpets, tearing out a wall, adding a shower to the half-bath off the kitchen. Our mother hated our house, our busy street, and was convinced if she could only update the floor plan, we'd be able to sell and move to a better neighborhood, meaning one she preferred, on a quieter street, in another town. I buried myself in my books, dreading the move and the loss of my friends.

One Sunday we took a rare break from the routine of Lewis and

me being locked out of the house while our parents cleaned up after the workmen and argued. We were going to Manhattan to have
brunch at my grandparents' favorite Chinese restaurant, Chun Cha
Fu on West 69th, to celebrate something. Good news, my grandfather had told my father over the phone. He'd tell us when we got
there.

We stopped by Ye-ye and Nai-nai's apartment on West 71st to
pick them up, but my grandfather wasn't waiting for us on the sidewalk. The commute from our house in New Jersey hadn't been particularly fast or slow this afternoon. We'd arrived fifty-five minutes after setting out on the Newark-Pompton Turnpike, but Ye-ye
wasn't there.

My father circled round the block once, then twice, and then my
mother said out loud what we'd all been thinking, "Hmm, that's
strange. I wonder where your father is."

Now with the words hanging in the air in the car, my heart beat
faster. I peered out the window for clues. But whereas clues always
popped up in obvious ways for Nancy Drew, teen detective, they
seemed nonexistent for me, Lu-ying Chiu, wannabe teen. Everything looked the same as every other Sunday, except for the Ye-ye-
sized hole in the universe.

I had wanted to show him my book, *Nancy Drew Number 57: The
Triple Hoax*. Ye-ye used to give me a dollar for every book I read until Dad made him stop in fourth grade, saying I was too old for that.
I didn't care; I didn't show Ye-ye my books for the cash. My father
didn't understand me at all.

One of the working girls on the stoops—my parents called them
"professionals," which confused me—perked up upon seeing our
large, boat-like Buick Electra creep down the block yet again. She
was thin and dressed casually in a yellow tube top and cut-offs,
it still being afternoon and not the usual working hours, but she

approached the curb cautiously. Then she saw my brother and me, faces anxiously peering out the back window, looking for Ye-ye, and she waved a hand dismissively and turned back to her stoop.

We sailed round the block, up West End Avenue, past the Jewish temple and senior center, then down Broadway—my father slowed so we could see if Ye-ye and Nai-nai were out walking—then he turned at the tiny corner McDonald's, inching back up to my grandparents' apartment building. My father set the blinkers, double-parking.

"Oh, George, don't stop here. There are some real pros by the steps." Mom pointed with a long finger.

My brother and I craned our necks to see but it was the same woman in the yellow top and her friend hanging out the window from our last trip around the block.

Dad didn't answer. He was scowling. He unlocked the doors with a click, then jumped out. "Move the car if you see any police," he told my mother, then he bounded over to the callbox.

Mom locked the doors again.

I watched from the backseat. I could hear the dial tone. It rang and rang. I couldn't remember a time when the loud BUZZ hadn't sounded the moment Dad touched the box. My brother was playing with his toy soldiers, making shooting sounds, "pshoo, pshoo," and wounded sounds, "aargh! aaaw!"

"Quiet, Lewis," I said. "I'm trying to hear. Roll down your window."

"Don't roll down the windows," Mom said from the front seat.

"Maaaaaa, I'm trying to hear."

My mother rolled down the window on her side a tiny bit.

The pros and pimps were calling to each other, there was a ringing sound, traffic, pigeons cooing.

After what seemed like forever, Dad came running out of the

building, red-faced, sweating. He threw open the car door; Mom barely had time to scoot over again. "Ye-ye's been hospitalized. His heart."

"Oh, George." My mother's face grew pale.

My father pulled out without looking, nearly hitting a yellow cab, which honked. The cabbie shouted out his window, "Asshole! You asshole! Whadyathink—" My father honked back, pounding the horn, over and over and over again, until the cabbie drove off.

"George! George!" Uncle Lincoln appeared on the sidewalk, shouting, his face as red as my father's.

My father turned and the two of them started shouting at each other in Chinese, then Uncle Lincoln jumped in the backseat, pushing Lewis into me. "Sorry, kids. Hey, kids, how you doing? George, George, look out. I haven't heard from Harry." Then they started shouting to each other in Chinese again. All I could recognize were their Chinese names: Hao-bo, Hao-hsin, Hao-hsueh. Only in English did their names really stand apart. Lewis and I were named after Uncle Lincoln, in fact. The L at any rate. Because he and Dad were always the closest despite their difference in age and because Dad helped Uncle Lincoln choose his American name. I got the Chinese name because I was eldest, the first of the family to be born in America, and clearly the experiment, while Lewis just got the L.

Lewis whispered in my ear, his breath hot and wet against my neck. "Uncle Lincoln has a perm."

"Sssh! I'm trying to listen," I said.

I peered around my brother. Uncle Lincoln's normally black, straight hair was now bent in stiff, orangeish curls like a wire sculpture of crispy noodles set atop his head.

Lewis pursed his lips together tightly, holding his tongue.

Uncle Lincoln leaned forward, holding onto the back of Dad's

seat, and shouted things I couldn't make out. He wasn't using sim-
ple words I understood, like the names of our family members, the
dishes we liked to eat, how to say "thank you" and "you're welcome"
and "shut up, Stupid Egg!" Dad was facing forward, but he wasn't
really looking at the street or at the honking cars, he was staring
into something unseeable and nodding.

I recognized the word for "Father" and "kitchen" and then Uncle
Lincoln shouted in English, "Operator! It's an emergency! Send an
ambulance!" He held an invisible phone to his ear, pantomiming.
"Quick! Quick! My father's lying on the kitchen floor."

"George, look at the road!" Mom said.

In the confusion it was as though the streets were an Escher
print, with moving pieces that coalesced, turning into something
unexpected. A delivery truck, double parked; two cop cars, lights
flashing; an elderly Jewish couple, jaywalking.

Dad turned back to the street and we lurched around the corner,
then onto Broadway, cars honking as we merged. Dad had a grim,
determined look on his face that meant he was going to ignore
them, and our large Buick Electra eased into the lane.

Finally, we pulled up to the white loading zone in front of Chun
Cha Fu. My father barely waited for us to get out of the car, before
pulling off with Uncle Lincoln, who was still shouting from the
backseat, repeating everything he'd seen, the shock of it, over and
over.

I followed my mother into the restaurant, a sick hollow feeling in
my stomach. Everything seemed strange. A waiter rushed up to us
with three menus, the English kind. If Ye-ye were there, they would
never have given us those.

Mom insisted the waiter take us to a side room, with the large
round table for families, as if everyone would be coming together
as usual.

"Well, we might as well sit down and wait," Mom smiled, pretending. I stared at the pages of my book, but I couldn't concentrate. I stared at a faint stain on the tablecloth. Oyster sauce, I figured. I never noticed the stains when Ye-ye and Nai-nai were here.

Then Aunt Marcie stormed through the dining room, steering a stroller between the tables. She was wearing one of the long polyester caftans she'd adopted as a uniform ever since her pregnancy. It had been six and a half months since the baby was born, but she was still dressing like that, like a flowered awning had attached itself to her body.

"Vivian!" she called too loudly. "Can you believe it?"

My cousin Margot trotted after her. She looked hot, her cheeks flushed, her limp, black hair sticking to her neck and face. Aunt Marcie believed in cutting Margot's hair very short; she said it would make it grow thicker that way. Margot was almost seven but small for her age. The short hair didn't help.

"Whath wrong with Ye-ye?" Margot lisped, sidling up to me. She set a Barbie on the tabletop. "I'm thared."

"What happened to your tongue?" I asked.

Margot sighed, rolling her large black eyes. "Ith thore." She opened her mouth and pulled her lower lip down so that I could see. There was a red plastic bead wedged in the gap between two of her baby teeth.

"How did you do that?"

Margot shook her head. "I wath playing with the baby on the floor, and it juth happened."

"Gross." Lewis wrinkled his nose.

"Don't make fun of Margot," I said. It was hard to keep track of the little kids and eavesdrop on the adults at the same time.

"I suppose we'll be the last to find out what's going on." Aunt Marcie flipped through the menu as though she actually planned to order something. "Where are the waiters?"

"As far as I can make out, Ye-ye has had a second heart attack." My mother shook her head.

"Uncle Lincoln found him on the kitchen floor," I interjected.

Mom and Aunt Marcie turned to stare.

"Poor Ye-ye," Mom said.

"Like I said, we'll be the last to know." Aunt Marcie put her hand in the air and actually snapped her fingers.

Now they're going to spit in our drinks, I thought. The way Uncle Lincoln always said he and Uncle Harry used to back when they had to wait tables in high school.

But the bad part was only beginning.

Aunt Marcie looked straight at Mom, as though she were just noticing the highlights, which Mom had just had redone. "My great-aunt Agatha went blonde, too. Just before she died."

Mom and Aunt Marcie didn't get along. Aunt Marcie was insecure, Mom said. She and Uncle Harry were going to get a divorce last year, but then Aunt Marcie had the baby and now they weren't. I knew because I'd overheard Mom on the phone with Aunt Marcie. Mom made me promise not to say anything.

I took a breath and held it until it hurt in my chest, pressing inside me like a dying balloon. There'd be a fight at home now. All the bad moments were converging, everything at once, like we couldn't hold them off anymore, as though there weren't enough good memories to keep the bad ones from winning. Mom and Dad would fight in the kitchen or worse in their bedroom and Mom would say she wanted to go back to her family in California, and Dad might shout, and she'd shout back, and glass would break, something small, a decorative vase, a picture frame, that red ashtray we used to have for guests. What small thing was left to break? I tried to remember from my dusting all the little tchotchkes in their bedroom. The purple glass perfume bottle. The blue clay plate from Laguna Beach that Dad kept his loose pocket change on. The giant conch shell we could all hear the ocean in. I didn't want anything else to break. We didn't have anything left that I wouldn't miss.

Mom put her hand on her hip, her sharp elbow pointed out.

Aunt Marcie pushed at her own permed black hair, as though to make a point.

But then the waiters came with short, sweaty glasses of water with ice and Mom ordered food for us from the English menu, which Ye-ye never used, and the fight somehow died before it could begin.

The baby woke up and made some gurgling baby noise.

Mom turned away from Aunt Marcie and bent toward it, remarking how sweet and beautiful it was.

I pressed my hands to a spot above my heart and held them there. As if. As if. As if.

TWO AND a half hours passed before Dad came bursting through the front doors, his mouth in a tight straight line. His concern made me feel nervous all over again.

"George, how is your father?" My mother stood up, and my father sat down, slumping.

My mother poured him some tea. He drank without looking at it.

"He's okay," Dad said. "No heart attack. Just palpitations."

"Thank God," my mother said.

Aunt Marcie stood up. "Where's Harry? Am I supposed to wait here forever?" She marched off toward the front door.

"How you doing, Margot?"

My cousin perked up, smiling. "I'm fine, thank you, Uncle George. Look at my tooth!" She pulled her lip down to reveal the bead.

"That's good, that's good," Dad said without looking. He ran his hand through his hair so that it stood on end. "The cardiologist is keeping Ba overnight for observation."

"How's your mother?" my mother asked.

"She's back in the apartment. Lincoln's staying with her."

"Uncle Lincoln's not coming?" I asked, disappointed.

"Lincoln's responsible. Or at least he feels responsible. He told Ma he's engaged. That was the good news."

"What?" Mom stood up.

The baby started crying.

"Oh, no. Not again." Margot covered her ears and put her head down on the table.

Aunt Marcie came back. She looked at her crying baby: "Like clockwork. I was beginning to leak." Aunt Marcie shook her head and felt for her own breasts through all the fabric of the caftan. "I'm a regular automat these days." She laughed in a way that showed she didn't think it was funny. She sat down heavily in one of the chairs.

"But Lincoln can't get married," Mom said.

"Who's Uncle Lincoln going to marry?" I asked and for once, like a miracle, my voice carried, above the whimpering baby, and the murmur of the restaurant, and the plates clattering, and the traffic outside. Dad turned to look at me like he'd just realized I was there.

"His secretary. The grad student."

"Mariceles?" Mom exclaimed. "He can't marry her."

"She's pregnant apparently," Dad said. "That was what caused the fight."

"Well, well, well, Lincoln's long bachelor days are finally coming to an end," Aunt Marcie said.

"But that can't be Lincoln's baby!" Mom was waving her hands in front of her as though she needed to create a wind that would put out a fire on the table. "I mean, I should know. I was his best friend. We were dating."

"You weren't dating." Dad shook his head.

"Well, yes, we were," Mom said angrily. "And I know Lincoln doesn't like her that way. He can't marry that-that-that *woman*. He's . . . " and she paused, before whispering loudly, *"you know."*

Then Uncle Harry came running in; he didn't even sit down. "I'm double parked!" he announced. "We have to go!"

"Well, you've missed the show, as usual," Aunt Marcie said. "Apparently we're the only two who've been out of the loop."

Then he noticed Aunt Marcie feeding the baby. "My god, Marcie, cover yourself." He took his jacket off and slung it over Aunt Marcie's shoulders.

"Don't worry about me. At least I'm natural."

"What is that supposed to mean?" Mom said.

Aunt Marcie stood up with the baby still hooked to her breast. "We should go, Harry. I, for one, am tired of being the last person on earth this family thinks about. To think, I let Lincoln babysit Margot while I was giving birth."

I didn't know why she was upset about that. Uncle Lincoln babysat all of us. He always brought us toys from Chinatown, snakes made out of bamboo, magic wooden boxes that made coins disappear, packs of cards with instructions on how to pull aces out of ears and hide hearts up our sleeves. He was our favorite babysitter.

Aunt Marcie didn't even wait to see if Margot was following her. She just walked out while Uncle Harry grabbed the stroller and ran after her.

BACK IN the car, Mom and Dad were fighting. Or rather, Mom was. She was angry. "What got into him?"

"I don't know. Maybe Lincoln figured Ba and Ma won't last forever and he thought he'd make them happy for once. Maybe this is another of his do-gooder projects. He's always trying to fix broken things and making things worse."

"Oh, George. That's awful to say."

"Anyway, Ba's going to be okay. But what a disaster." Dad sighed.

It turned out Nai-nai had been upset about the engagement. Not because Mariceles was already pregnant without them being married, but because, Dad said, she was Puerto Rican and not Chinese.

"Mom's not Chinese," I said from the backseat.

"Yes, but she's white."

"Nai-nai is prejudiced," Lewis declared, in the way that little kids can just blurt things out, and a silence fell over the car. I wanted Dad to say something else, like *Yes, and we will all stand behind Lincoln and Mariceles because Nai-nai is wrong*, but he didn't say it. My parents' silences about many things alarmed me. They made me aware of invisible lines that I couldn't see that they drew between themselves and the rest of the world. I never knew when that line might be drawn to exclude me.

THE NEXT month everything in the family changed. We didn't meet for Sunday brunch at all. There was too much fighting. Uncle Harry and Aunt Marcie announced they were boycotting the wedding. Aunt Marcie had just gotten a gig as the organist at St. Anne's. She wasn't even Catholic. At best she was a lukewarm Lutheran, but she said, "How would it look?"

And Uncle Harry wasn't talking to us at all. Mom said he'd been in denial. It wasn't her fault that she'd spilled Uncle Lincoln's secret. No one told Ye-ye or Nai-nai why everyone was fighting, so Nai-nai assumed the family was taking sides, for and against Mariceles. She wrote long letters to my father, with pictures of various Chinese girls that she'd solicited from friends, from other old ladies at her senior center, her old missionary acquaintances, who knows where else.

"Ugh, what a mess," Dad said, when he said anything at all. Mostly he buried himself in his schoolwork, refusing to answer the phone or come to dinner on time. He had taken over the family room for his study, his piles of notes and typed pages spreading across the two folding tables and the end table, so Lewis and I weren't allowed there anymore either, which meant there was no more TV for us that summer. We were confined to the backyard or our own rooms until the house was finished, which seemed an ever dicier proposition.

I couldn't even have tuned in to *Soap* if I'd wanted to. I had no idea where to turn for more information, for guidance. I didn't feel like this situation was something I could talk to my friends about. I was left to stew in my own ignorance, my Nancy Drew mysteries providing no clues whatsoever.

"TO THINK," Mom said, "I could've married him someday if I'd only known!" She said this several times a week, at dinner, or in the car while we were driving to the grocery store, and once before breakfast during the middle of the *Today* show. I had the TV on in the kitchen because Gene Shalit was going to talk to Pamela Sue Martin, and I refused to leave for school until I saw the interview. I'd become obsessed with Ms. Martin, her dark red hair, her sleepy eyes, the voice like a girl who'd just gotten up no matter what time of day she was speaking. I didn't have words yet for the way I felt about her. That, too, was a mystery.

Dad had already left for work, and it was just the three of us around the table.

Mom said, "It's not that I don't love your father. But I never realized I had a chance with Lincoln."

She sighed in a long dramatic way.

"But then you wouldn't have us," Lewis said.

"Oh, I'd have children like you," Mom said, quickly, and then she laughed. *Ha ha ha.* Dramatic and deliberate. "I'm just kidding. I love you very much." She pulled Lewis close to her and kissed him on the top of his head.

THAT SEPTEMBER, school started and our house was still in disrepair. I hoped that meant we might not really move and I might be able to stay with my friends. Junior high began just like any year in elementary school for me, except *Nancy Drew Mysteries* was cancelled on TV and all my friends started reading Trixie Belden.

Dad took over the ping pong table for his books as the construction spread to the basement, and that meant no more ping pong for Lewis and me. My skills got rusty, and Gertrude Harter was able to beat me in gym class, 11–9, 13–11, 11–7.

Then at the last minute, just before Christmas, Lincoln announced the engagement was called off. Mariceles's old boyfriend came back, and at first Mom thought that meant Mariceles would marry him. But instead Mariceles told Lincoln she found marriage to be a bourgeois establishment affectation to oppress women, and she had decided to stay single.

Uncle Lincoln moved to the West Coast after that. To California.

"I wish we could all go with him," Mom said.

THE FAMILY had started getting together again, even if there was a Lincoln-shaped hole in our universe. Nai-nai liked to bring his letters to read bits out loud, as though he were seated at the table still, so his brothers could hear how he was doing. He'd found a couple of teaching jobs at a community college, nothing tenure-track yet, and one Sunday Nai-nai announced proudly that he was running a Saturday enrichment program for at-risk youth.

Uncle Harry said, "Lincoln is a pervert. They should keep him away from children." He said this loudly enough for us to hear at the kids' table to the side.

None of the other adults said anything after that. Silence fell over the table and the congealing plates of brown sauce long beans and half-eaten moo goo gai pan. Soon it was time to leave, to drop Nai-nai and Ye-ye back at their apartment. Nobody was hungry enough to order a final soup.

Dad said that Uncle Harry had always been jealous because Lincoln was the youngest. After Lincoln was born, he felt he never got any attention.

Mom cried all the way home, through the grim traffic in the Lincoln Tunnel. I watched the condensation dripping down the stained tile walls, and Lewis wondered aloud what kept the water of the Hudson from seeping inside and drowning us all.

I didn't say anything, but I felt the problem was that no one in the family had learned to stand up to Uncle Harry's bullying. He was considered the clever one, the successful businessman, and he had the most money, which intimidated my grandparents into thinking he was something they should be proud of.

After that, we didn't get together so much.

NAI-NAI AND Uncle Lincoln remained close, however. Over the years, they gossiped over the phone long-distance. Ye-ye complained about the phone bill, but there was nothing he could do. A mother must talk to her son, she told him.

I envied them. Mom had found my VHS copies of *Battlestar Galactica* and *Blade Runner* and thrown them in the trash. Drawn to their smoky eyes, I taped pictures of Maren Jensen and Sean Young torn from magazines next to my mirror. Mom took me to volunteer at church, washing dishes every Sunday during the donut social after Mass. She made me work with her after school and volunteer on Saturdays. I was too busy to go to movies with my friends, so I might as well have moved, I never got to see them anymore. I never had time even to watch TV, even though Pamela Sue Martin was now on *Dallas* every Wednesday night.

I did not understand many things: why my mother seemed intent on punishing me while my brother was allowed to keep crumpled girlie magazines in his closet as though we didn't both know they were there; why I had more chores than he; why he was allowed to stay out late and I was expected to do the dishes and clean the house and keep up my grades on top of work and church. My mother complained that I did not even resemble her, as though I were growing my hair straight and dark deliberately to spite her. I seemed to be punished for having been born female, as though she wanted to extract some penance for her own life having turned out nothing as she had once imagined. I did not understand why I found both girls and boys attractive, but not all, not always, and never the boys my mother liked, the ones who carried her groceries to the car, the ones who attended her Bible study classes. I could not imagine my mother ever dating Uncle Lincoln. I could not imagine her as a young woman with dreams.

WHEN I was in high school, Uncle Lincoln wrote a long op-ed that was published in the *Los Angeles Times*. He sent copies to Dad, to

Mom, to Uncle Harry and Aunt Marcie even. Uncle Lincoln and his partner, Rafael, were running a clinic to offer free tests for HIV, and together they'd denounced Reagan's silence on AIDS.

Mom said, "So it's official."

Dad said, "Good for Lincoln."

But nobody translated the article for my grandparents. I don't know if they ever saw it, if they knew what a good person Lincoln was.

JUST BEFORE my high school graduation, Nai-nai died in her sleep. Everyone had thought Ye-ye would be the first to go. We went to her funeral instead of my commencement.

Uncle Lincoln was despondent. He shaved his head, he refused to eat, he said he wanted to move back to New York to take care of Ye-ye.

"You were an impeccable son," Mom told him, over and over, at the funeral banquet, while he sat in a daze at the table, unable to greet any of Ye-ye and Nai-nai's old friends who'd come to pay their respects. "You loved your mother."

It made me envious to see how solicitous Mom was over Uncle Lincoln's feelings. And it made me wonder what it would feel like to love a mother the way Uncle Lincoln loved Nai-nai.

WHEN I was twenty-seven, Mom died, too, after a short and brutal fight with breast cancer. She was fifty-six. She and I had been fighting for years, and this continued until the very end. Uncle Lincoln was the one who helped Dad find the burial plot, make the funeral arrangements, notify the papers. Dad was practically catatonic with grief. He'd believed up to the end there'd be a miracle that would save her.

Lincoln put together an album for me. "*In Remembrance*," it said in gold script across the red cover. Inside it was filled with pictures of Mom and Uncle Lincoln together, dressed up for concerts, Lincoln in black tie, Mom in slinky dresses that sparkled. She'd never dressed up like that with Dad. Lincoln stood up very straight, so that he'd appear taller, and Mom posed with a hand on her hip, one knee bent, another behind her head, smiling. She looked like a movie star. I had never seen my mother look happier.

"He was a perfect gentleman," Mom had said once. The perfect date for a chaste Catholic girl.

AFTER THE funeral, Dad was too upset to talk, and Lewis and his wife were trying to comfort him. I sat in a lorazepam-induced haze at the table in the basement of St. Anne. The church ladies were clearing up the lunch.

Uncle Lincoln sidled up to me, the album in hand. "You know, Lu-ying, we Chinese have the Day of the Dead, too. More than one. It's going to be up to you to remember this. Don't let your father forget."

Then he told me about Qing Ming, Clear Brightness, for sweeping the tombs and leaving food on graves in remembrance of dead family members, and Gui Jie, Ghost Festival, for burning incense and fake money for ghosts to spend in the afterlife. He'd written these things down for me on a sheet of lined paper.

"Your mother was Catholic, and your father will remember the Catholic things, but I'm telling you, so you'll remember the Chinese ones, too."

Sometimes it irritated me how forgiving Lincoln was, how much he cared about the things Mom cared about, how unquestioning his loyalty was. "Mom wasn't Chinese," I said dully.

"That's not true. She was part of the family," Lincoln said. "She was always more interested in keeping the traditions than the rest of us. Ye-ye and Nai-nai appreciated that about your mother."

Then he held up the album he'd put together.

"Don't forget," he said. "Be sure to pick a good photo and put it on an altar. Light a candle. Put a bowl of fruit, fresh fruit, so you have to change it. Don't get the plastic kind."

I took the album from him, pried it from his fingers, and Lincoln finally unclenched, sitting down heavily in a folding chair next to mine. He sat as though his bones were melting into the metal.

My mother had been correct about one thing. Uncle Lincoln had loved her. Not in the way she could understand, nor in the way that she had wanted, but this was love, too. And in her own way, Mom had loved Lincoln.

I looked across the room at my father, but he was absorbed in the antics of my newborn niece, the first child of Lewis and his wife, Julie. Waves of bitterness and anger and jealousy swept over my body.

After all those fights with Mom growing up, the way she used her church as a cudgel, I found I still wanted to hurt her. I wanted to wound even her ghost. What had kept me from partnering up, not with Luce, there were other issues, but perhaps with Pei, if not my mother's many contradictory and onerous rules for love?

I took a deep breath and tried to release it slowly.

It was still easier for me to blame my mother than to consider my own messiness. If I were honest, I'd admit that she had been as confused as anyone. And I was not good at recognizing love and acceptance even when it sat at my table.

When I had calmed, I put my hand on Uncle Lincoln's back. I could feel his heart beating through his bones and flesh and dark, wool suit jacket.

Perhaps it was my touch that released something within him because finally he bent his head over his hands and cried, tears streaming down his cheeks. I didn't know how to console him.

"These were our salad days," he said, gesturing to the album on the table between us. "We were just figuring things out."

I nodded, promising that I'd remember, on the Chinese days of the dead and all the other days, too. Not everyone, almost no one, had his capacity to love with such a clear and luminous heart. Uncle Lincoln deserved to have someone honor his memories, his loyalty, his unique and precious gift. "I won't forget," I said, and took his hand in mine.

THE BODY

THE CRANE OPERATOR

A gray mist like a shroud hung over the construction site of the future Happy Prosperity Shopping Center as the morning crew set to work. The crane operator rode the elevator to his position in the top of the crane, then waited while he watched the line of migrants filing in. They would clear the rubble by hand with shovels and buckets and wheelbarrows. They were skinny and filthy and were brought in by truck from whatever wretched dormitory the company housed them in. At least the crane operator had that much to be grateful for: he wasn't fresh out of the countryside, he'd been able to buy an apartment after fifteen years of construction jobs, he had a wife, they were having a baby. He'd been lucky to come when he did. Not that he didn't like to complain. Complaining meant he had something to lose.

"This smog will kill us all," Lao Bing complained to his partner over the mic. He pulled the loops of his hospital-grade face mask up tighter over his ears. "My wife wants me to buy a new air filter. Her friends have something fancy from Korea. Cost more than two thousand yuan. I said, 'What do the Koreans know about air pollution? Hai'er's good enough for me.' You know what she said? 'If you're a man, you'd be willing to buy this for our daughter.' She's pulling that trick."

A voice buzzed in his ear. "You should tell her, 'If I'm not a man, how did you get pregnant?'"

"I told her I've already worked sixty hours overtime this month. Why doesn't she get her parents to give her the money for their precious granddaughter?"

"If it's not the smog, it's the overtime. One way or the other, we're all dead men," his partner concurred genially.

"Shut up and get to work," their boss shouted over the mic, but good-naturedly. They laughed. The routine, day after day, was the same.

He turned on the ignition and began the code sequence for the giant crane. It let out a loud *beep-beep-beep* as he backed the machine over the bumpy, uneven ground.

If only the wind would pick up, he thought. *Blow some of this smog away.* When he was a child, he remembered waking up to his mother blowing gently across his face, trying to dislodge the flakes of coal that had settled there overnight. Henan was a coal-producing province, and his mother had always said they were lucky to have the fuel to make it through the winter. She still remembered the shortages of her youth, when one winter they'd had to burn the furniture—meaning the family's wooden kitchen table, their stools, the frame to their lone, shared bed—to keep from freezing. And still her hands had bled every day from the cold.

It was March. Soon enough the weather would be warmer, and people would stop burning so much coal.

Although with the factories these days and their crazy production schedules, it was hard to tell. Spring used to be a time of clearing air. But the crane operator remembered how smoggy it had been in August. In his youth August had been a dry, dusty month of clear blue skies, a time when the old men played the *erhu* on the edge of the paddies, the notes slipping over the green fields of rice, sorghum, and corn. All the mothers and fathers walked on dirt paths carrying giant dippers of water to their crops, praying no sudden freak storm would arise and crush their fields with hail before the September harvest. As a child, it had been a time of complete freedom, running barefoot through the village, chasing his friends or hunting gophers with a slingshot. It had been his favorite time of the year, better even than the New Year with its fireworks, gifts of candy, and red envelopes of lucky cash.

Now every month was gray, choked with gray clouds that made his eyes and throat burn, his chest tightening with every breath.

"All clear."

The crane operator flicked the switch for the wrecking ball. His muscles tensed, his jaw tightened. Fifteen years on construction and he still imagined he could feel it in his body the moment the giant iron ball struck concrete.

CRASH

The air shook around him as the ball hit the wall. Dust rose up, thicker even than the fog, like an avalanche of concrete. His crane beeped as he backed up to wait while the dust cleared before he struck again.

Beep. Beep. Beep.

"Good hit," his partner's voice crackled in his earpiece. "One more fifteen degrees west and this next one's coming down."

"Got it." He squinted at his control panel. If anything, the day was getting darker as the morning progressed. He reset the coordinates and hit the gas pedal.

"What the—?" his partner's voice was in his ear. "Idiot farmers are running toward the building again. Hold on. Can't tell what's happening. It's all *luan qi ba zao.*"

"Tell them you'll fire them! I can't waste time—"

There was a crackle of static. The crane operator looked over his shoulder, trying to see through the haze. It seemed that the migrants were indeed approaching again but this time at a run, and one of the crazies was waving his shovel over his head.

"What's the matter?"

"STOP! CUT YOUR ENGINE! There's a body!"

"Where, where?"

The crane operator hit the emergency brake. His heart pounded in his chest. He hoped one of the bumpkin idiots hadn't got in the way after all. He'd be blamed. He'd lose his job. Like that, his luck would evaporate. Nothing. Gone. Now this. Now something.

"What's happened?"

"It's a woman," his partner's voice crackled in his ear. "You'd better come down and look at this."

Like that, he felt a stab of ice shoot through his body. He knew in an instant, less than a heartbeat, his luck could change.

THE REPORTER

The woman's body was covered with a tarp by the time the reporter arrived at the construction site, but at least the corpse hadn't been removed. Her editor was adamant that she see the body with her own eyes.

There were police cars parked in clumps along the street leading up to the site and several unmarked passenger cars, which she assumed had to be undercover security officials. Li Ming had to show her press association card and work ID to the officers guarding the entrance to the site. Then she had to show them again to the site foreman inside. He was sweating profusely, perspiration beading across his forehead underneath his hard, yellow helmet, despite the fact it was a cool day for March, the smog blocking the sun almost entirely. As she walked behind the foreman to the site where the body had been found, she couldn't help but feel sorry for him. A bad luck thing like this happening on his watch. Even though it wasn't his fault, his bosses might find a way to blame him.

"We follow all safety regulations carefully," the foreman chattered as he stepped over the furrows in the ground. "We use every known official precaution before all demolitions."

Li followed him across the uneven ground littered with broken cinder blocks, bricks, dirt, empty soda cans, and ramen and snack wrappers. Through the gloom, she could make out a cluster of men hunched on the edge of a half-demolished apartment building. A green tarpaulin had been placed over what she assumed must be the body.

Three cops were typing into computer tablets. A fourth stood watch by the tarp. He was smoking and looking off into the distance, or at least into the thick fog.

The foreman called out to the cops. "There's another reporter wants to see the body."

Her heart sunk. One of her competitors had beaten her here.

But the cop didn't even glance her way. He gestured for one of his underlings to pull back the tarp, and sure enough one of the younger cops immediately broke from the cluster and dutifully trotted over. Li Ming guessed from their casual attitude the cops didn't consider the case politically sensitive. Or even that important.

She figured that meant the victim was poor.

Then the cop pulled back the tarp, and despite wanting to seem tough and seasoned and competent, she couldn't help but gasp.

"Yeah, get a load of her," the first cop said. "What a shame."

Li pulled her notebook out of her purse and began writing.

The body was naked, female, less bruised than one would imagine for someone who was found amidst rubble. (Note: The dead woman was not killed by a falling building. But then how had she died? Perhaps she had already been dead.) She appeared young, in her late teens or early twenties. The corpse's skin tone was ashen, bluish almost, and not a color Li was used to seeing on an actual person. Her stomach flipped and tightened, and she could taste her breakfast, rice congee, a fried egg.

Pale body but darker face and neck, which suggested the dead woman had worked outdoors or was from the countryside. She had shoulder-length hair, black roots but lighter brown halfway down, as though she'd been lightening her hair for a while then gave up. Her face was without makeup, her eyebrows bushy, full lips, wide-ish nose with a very low bridge. There was something about her that said "countryside." Maybe a stockiness to the body, thick legs, strong arms. Someone who was used to working. Not a thin, delicate city girl. But perhaps Li was prejudiced, having grown up in a village. She had the same type of body as this woman, was stronger than she looked, and it was a point of pride. But who knew? It was possible for a city girl to be strong as well, Li supposed. The dead woman was taller than Li, maybe 1.75 meters. She had dirt on her arms and legs in thick swathes; then Li realized, no, it wasn't dirt. She had dark bruises, almost black, and then discoloration, a reddish-purple so dark it only seemed like bruises, around both wrists and both ankles.

Li looked at the rest of the body. The dead woman's breasts lay flattened against her ribs. Li tried to lean closer to see if she had any distinguishing marks, moles or freckles or scars, but there was nothing visible along the torso.

"Are you allowed to turn her over? May I see her back?"

"Why you want to do that for? Her face not good enough for you?" the young police officer snickered.

"In case she has a scar or a birthmark or something unusual on her back. Something her family might recognize if I describe it in the paper."

"Good idea," said the foreman. "You see, we are fully cooperating with the authorities. Can you have your assistants turn over the body?"

"Oh." The officer gestured for two of his underlings to come forward. "Turn her over. The reporter needs to see the back of the body."

The men raised their eyebrows, and then they pulled gloves out of their pockets and put them on. They gingerly took hold of the body by the hands and feet and turned her over.

There on the upper left shoulder blade was a strange black symbol, a tattoo that appeared to have been crudely cut into the skin: not an actual character, but a strange, uneven rectangle about four centimeters long and three centimeters high with a triangle inside and three slanted lines radiating from the top and sides of the rectangle.

Was that some kind of Falun Gong or other cult symbol? Li wondered. She sketched the design carefully in her notebook.

Was she a suicide? Some kind of doomsday thing? Or a gesture of protest?

This was the kind of detail that could make a story a sensation, especially if her competitor had not noticed. Something a family might recognize, something a crime ring might be using to identify its members (usually tattoos were for men, but exciting if women were joining in the trend), or something that could be used to rally the public against a dangerous cult. Li briefly imagined a promotion, an offer to work for CCTV, an exciting turn of good fortune that would please her parents after what had otherwise been a lackluster career in a seemingly dead-end job at one of the lesser provincial papers.

Apart from the crude tattoo, there were no other distinguishing marks, nor anything that suggested how the woman had died. She clearly had not been crushed to death by anything falling on her. Instead her body had merely been revealed when part of the building was destroyed.

There were no cuts or other wounds on her. Her face was not contorted. She lay almost peacefully, the body in relatively good shape, apart from being dead.

Her body appeared, Li didn't know how else to describe it, but almost *too clean.*

"May I take a picture? Not for the paper, but for my notes?" Li asked the officer in charge and pulled out her small digital camera from her purse.

"No way," he said. And waved a white-gloved hand in her face.

"I promise we won't print it. I just want to make sure I get all the details right—"

"If your eyes aren't good enough . . . ," and he pushed her camera away.

"But Older Brother, my boss will want me to write a very detailed account. Even a small thing that my eyes can't notice might help a family identify this girl."

"Her family will hide their heads in shame," the cop said. "Look at her! Naked and dead. What kind of family would want to claim her? She's probably a prostitute and she's been killed by her pimp because she tried to hide her money or else run away."

"We can't know that—"

"Why else is she naked?"

"How would I know? Maybe she was robbed!"

The cop snorted, a loud pig-like grunt. "Maybe she was. But who wants to steal clothes? You know what I think, it was some kind of pervert. Followed her from work, then forced her to come here to this abandoned site and raped her, took all her clothes, and killed her. All the same, her family will still be ashamed. We'll be lucky if we can ever identify her. And the only way her family will come forward is if we can find them first before they go into hiding and force them to pay for the disposal of the body. Mark my words."

As the man argued, Li was able to take a quick shot of the body. It would appear in tomorrow's paper, along with the headline: Mysterious Beauty Found Dead. The photo, cropped to reveal only the woman's face and shoulders, would appear above the fold. The issue would sell out within an hour.

LI WOULD not get a promotion. She would not get a call from any better-paid news organizations. However, her editor was indeed pleased, and she would be assigned to re-write every sordid crime story that crossed his desk. She had a great eye for detail, he said.

THE ITINERANT PRIEST

Itinerant Priest Mo Xugui rummaged through the fruit on the corner of Jiefang Road and Geming Boulevard, his favorite stand in the city. Let the pretentious shop at the new markets with their waxed produce, polished into a fine gloss like plastic toys, but he preferred to buy from the farmers who still made it into the city, their produce piled in the backs of their carts. He wanted to smell the dirt, see it flake off the skin of the carrots and turnips and giant heads of *bai cai* cabbage before he bought his produce. He was a wood sign, creative, and soil gave him strength.

Fruit bought on the street was also cheaper. He tried to hit the stands late in the afternoon, when the poor farmers were beginning to lose hope and might start to pack up, head to whatever hovel they rented for cheap until they could go back to their village again. At night the sidewalk stands catered to the savory crowd, the drunks coming out of karaoke bars, the young workers with time on their hands, people who wanted hot bowls of noodles or fried pig ears and peppers. Mo timed his shopping to coincide with the long shadows that slid down the sidewalks like an evening tide, when the air grew cooler, when the farmers were most likely to bargain, the long day weighing on their already weary bones. He had a good eye for fatigue. He swept up to the old man seated on a wooden stool, kumquats and pomelos in hand-made baskets on a red-and-blue plastic tarp. The old man's eyes were rheumy, half-closed, and he'd put his hands into his sleeves to keep them warm. Just the kind of man who'd agree to half price, maybe 75 percent off to get rid of his merchandise and head inside for the evening.

"Long day," Mo called out to the farmer. "A blessing for you who labors so hard."

Mo placed his hands together and recited rapidly a few lines of Daoist text in their classical form.

The farmer looked up.

"How about a good price, and I'll take your fruit so you can go rest?"

The old man rubbed his back, and Mo knew he'd agree to his price.

Mo watched as the weary farmer weighed his kumquats, then slid the orange fruit into a cone made from the daily newspaper. Mo took the cone, rubbed a kumquat against his black robe, and then popped it into his mouth.

He was halfway through the fruit when his eye caught sight of the lurid crime story: "Mysterious Beauty Found Dead."

He read the article carefully and discovered the description of the tattoo. A sign of a black tantric Buddhist sect popular in some of the poorer mountain villages. Well, that meant there would be no money forthcoming from the family if they even knew their daughter/sister/wife had been killed. Poor people would keep to themselves. It was almost enough to make him toss the paper.

Then he recognized the address.

A rapidly changing neighborhood. Many older buildings that had housed families for generations were being torn down, which meant undoubtedly bribes had changed hands. Someone important was spending and receiving money to displace so many families. Such people were richer than a god. He tried to remember what was being built. An office building? Something for foreigners? Then he remembered. A shopping center. What bad luck for a property for a dead body to be found now. And naked. The worst kind of crime. The most unhappy of spirits. The kind that would likely haunt a place, bringing misfortune to all the shoppers who might tread on the site of its body's last breath.

Mo immediately understood the nature of the headaches that had been plaguing him for weeks. A new soul lost in the city calling to him.

He'd go to the site tomorrow morning. Bring his drum and his incense and start praying for the girl's lost soul. He'd shout loudly so that she could hear him above the howling winds and weeping ghosts on the other side.

And if the construction foreman tried to stop him, he'd explain his premonitions and his headaches and the long-term cost of a wandering soul who has died a violent death and how terrible this would be for business. Then he'd name his price for performing a full Daoist ceremony to make sure the girl's soul would leave for good.

Mo rubbed his hands together to dry the sticky juices from the kumquats. Already he could sense his vitality returning. An unfortunate death on a prosperous property. Exactly what he needed.

THE MIGRANT WORKER

At night in the room he shared with eleven other men, Xiao Jun no longer dreamed of his village tucked into the side of Song Mountain surrounded by pines, including one ancient tree that hung off the side of the mountain, its claw-like branches extended into the mist or sunlight or clouds so that the tree seemed like a dragon, coiled around the precipice. He did not dream of the sound of the ducks in Old Mrs. Meng's pond or the crowing of his grandfather's roosters or the snorting of the hogs the entire village used to raise for cash until there were no young people left to manage the work and the old heads left behind were too weak, bones too brittle to do it themselves. The last hog had been sold the year before. He had returned briefly for three days for Lunar New Year to bring presents and cash, for his grandparents and his young sisters. His parents had not returned that year; they had left when he was eight to work in the biggest factories in southern China, and they'd returned at first every year but then only occasionally. They said their bosses wouldn't pay them, wouldn't give the time off, but other parents returned to check on their left-behind children. Xiao Jun wasn't sure if his parents were telling the truth. He used to study hard so that his grandparents could brag about his marks and make his parents feel guilty about leaving such a diligent child, but after they stopped coming home at all and he took on more chores for his grandparents, it was harder to make top marks, and then the teacher left, and Xiao Jun stopped bothering to study.

He stopped dreaming of his grandmother's cooking, of the steaming bowls of hand-pulled noodles and patiently wrapped half-moon dumplings, the freshly pickled cabbage in the smooth rice porridge, the fried pig ears and peppers, the velvety spinach, the slivered carrots, the long dried green beans with cubes of tender *doufu*.

Instead for a long time, more than a year and three months, he dreamed the sleep of the dead, coming back from the construction crews where he picked up broken concrete and copper wires and lead pipes and chunks of other debris and loaded it into wheelbarrows. Sometimes he pushed the wheelbarrow from one end of a dirt field to deposit its contents on the other end in a new growing mountain of debris, and sometimes he broke the chunks of broken buildings further with a pick ax or a shovel or a strong piece of pipe. On some sites he'd been made to climb up the sides of buildings to wash windows of newly built skyscrapers, sitting on the edge of a rocking wood plank while the wind whistled in his ears, his legs wet from the squeegee dripping in his hand and the bucket of soapy water at his side. In the beginning he'd been afraid of falling; there were no nets, spider workers like him didn't need nets. He knew if he fell, it would be considered his fault and the bosses would be more pleased to be rid of him outright than forced to pay for nets that might catch his body before it hit the pavement below. But later he learned to watch the clouds float by on the glass in front of him. Sometimes he could imagine he was flying, and sometimes he could imagine that instead he was swimming in the vast bowl of the sky, the clouds reflected before him, the noise and filth of the city lost below.

But now on this job, he was back to picking up debris, and his body hurt in both new and familiar ways.

For months he'd slept with no dreams at all, his body so tired he fell into a black pool of nothingness the moment his body hit his cot, oblivious to the snores and farts and honking wheezing noises of the men sleeping in the bunks around him.

Then he'd found the girl's body.

She was young, maybe his age, seventeen, or maybe a few years older, but beautiful, even in death. Not bruised and damaged, not broken the way he would have expected a body to be amidst the rubble. Her skin was pale. Her hair long and black like a crow. Her lips full, the nose straight. She had sharp clavicles. And full breasts. He hadn't meant to see them, but she was naked, lying there.

At first, he thought she was asleep. He'd imagined she was homeless, a poor migrant girl, someone like himself, a girl from a village who was lost in the city, and she'd gone to sleep in the empty building, a deep tired sleep, and she hadn't heard the noise, and the wrecking ball had struck the old apartment building, and she'd died before she could even wake, lost in her dreams of her village.

But one of the men who'd almost graduated from high school before he'd left his village had seen a newspaper, and he claimed the reporter said the girl had not been killed by the crane. She'd already been dead. The crane had merely opened up the floor of the building where her body had been stashed. Fresh. Recently killed.

The other men had laughed salaciously. A wild chicken, they claimed. A prostitute no doubt. Why else was she naked?

Xiao Jun had blushed when he heard them, not out of shame, but out of anger. He felt protective of the girl whose body he'd found, his sharp eyes catching sight of the pallor of her flesh against the jumble of broken walls.

Other men had scaled the building, pulled her body out, brought it to the field, laid it there until the police could come, but he'd been the first to see her. Even though he'd never touched her flesh, it was to him that her ghost returned every night.

He was not asleep.

The first time she had arrived, he had not worked for three days. First the police had closed down the construction site to conduct their investigation, which the other men understood to be a ruse to force the owner of the construction company and the owner of the shopping center that they were building to come up with enough bribe money to make the investigation go in their favor. And then the Daoist priest arrived with his gongs and drums and incense and firecrackers and wails that let every passing pedestrian know that someone had died and now this was an unlucky site and they might catch the spirit's unhappiness, too. This continued on and off for two days until the police came and roughed up the priest. On the third day, the priest returned, but the foreman paid him off himself rather than call the police. Maybe paying the priest was cheaper than paying the police. Xiao Jun didn't know. At any rate, he knew the priest was a fraud. He was no one who could help the girl's unhappy ghost. He knew because the ghost was still there despite the man's gongs and drums and firecrackers and loud wails.

During those three days that he did not work but merely stood around or squatted with the other men, waiting to be told when to go back to work, he also did not sleep.

He lay in the dark of the crowded noisy room, and as much as he wanted to fall asleep and try to dream of his village or his grandparents or his younger sisters' faces, or even to fall into the deep dark black pit of nothingness and awake the next morning feeling that he'd not slept at all with only the cold and weight of work on his bones, he could not sleep.

He stared into the darkness and then suddenly she was there.

She stood before his bed.

She was naked just as he'd found her, but he could barely make out the contours of her body. She shimmered, her mouth opening and closing, but he could not hear her voice, he could not understand what she said. He lay in terror, rigid, afraid to move a muscle, a finger, a toe, until at last she disappeared without a sound, and all that was left of her visit was his erect penis to remind him that she had been there at all.

The next night she spoke again, or at least she opened and closed her mouth, but he still couldn't make out any sound. Her face was neutral, no sign of distress, neither fear nor anger nor sadness. Her eyes were open and seemed to stare directly at him.

"What do you want?" he called out. He hoped the other men would hear, would awaken and see her too and cry out and make her go away.

The moment he shouted, she disappeared. The other men did not wake up.

The third night, she appeared at the end of his bunk, the same as the previous two nights, and he sat up, less afraid now that she was more familiar. He'd been waiting, hoping she'd come. He leaned closer so that he could see better, try to understand what she was trying to say. But this night the ghost didn't stop at the end of his bed. She climbed onto his thin cotton mattress, and he pulled the sheets open for her instinctively, not because she was naked, but because she seemed as though she might be cold. And she was cold. Not like the draft from the window that never quite closed, but cold like water, like the lake outside his village where he used to swim with his classmates late at night after his grandparents had gone to sleep, and he and his friends would run in the dark, giggling, past the rice paddies and the sleeping ducks and the water buffalo that stood sleepily in the ditches alongside the dirt roads, through the reeds and the mud until splash, they were screaming with delight in the cold water that sucked the air out of his lungs, and his legs pumped in the water, kicking, his arms splashing, as he dove up and down in the lake like a boy turned fish, feeling free for the only time in his seventeen years of life.

That cold enveloped him now as the ghost straddled his body and his heart beatbeatbeat in his chest, and he rocked with the girl, her cold body over his warm one, she cooled the ache in his bones, the swollen purple bruises on his tan skin, back and forth, like waves they rocked together, until all the pain in his body had seeped into the ice and was gone.

THE DEVELOPER

The next morning the body lay in the bunk, lifeless.

The rumors spread quickly. An illness. A plague. Bad luck. Ever since they found that woman's body. Something contagious.

The men were restless, agitated.

The developer knew it could have been anything. Twenty years in the business, Zhang Xueke had seen it all. Heart attacks, brain aneurysms, drugs, suicide. Workers were unreliable, their bodies apt to fail in an infinite variety of ways.

When some of the men began to blame a ghost, evil spirits, drawn by the dead woman's body, saying it was bad luck that wouldn't go away, Zhang knew it was time to act.

The Daoist had disappeared out of the neighborhood, taken his money and run, and for all the men knew, maybe he'd conjured something to the site, something unholy, something vengeful.

The reporter had dug up something about a human trafficking ring that tattooed its victims so they could keep track of who owed what debts, young women lured from distant villages with promises of good-paying jobs in the city and then sold into brothels or mining towns or otherwise undesirable locations.

It was all sordid and bad for business.

Zhang closed the site down, moved the crew away, fired the

most vocal of the men as well as the older men, the kind with aches and pains, slower, liabilities really. He told his foreman to keep the hardest workers, the men who learned to shut up quickly and get on with it. He paid to have them moved to a new dormitory, a new site. He'd have to take the loss.

But he didn't give up. Zhang had paid dearly for the rights to develop the property; the thought of how many banquets he'd hosted, how many watches and cars and girls and promises had changed hands gave him migraines, exploding pain right behind his eyes, as though someone were drilling directly into his skull with sharp metal spikes. He had dependents, a wife, two spoiled children whose educations abroad were increasingly expensive, a mistress, but more importantly he had his reputation. If he lost face now, he could lose everything. Not just wealth, but liberty. Next time someone needed to take the fall for a deal gone bad, a new official rising through the ranks claiming to care about corruption, it could be Zhang who was charged, sentenced, imprisoned. There was only one way to survive in this world, and it was to succeed.

He hired a contingent of Buddhist monks to chant before the gates, no more of those tricky Daoists, found them in the government-subsidized monastery, realized he should have done this from the outset. Zhang paid men to set off firecrackers, more than one hundred strings to scare away the superstitious. He ordered that the lights be left on in the dormitories 24/7. If the men were afraid of the dark, let them sleep in the light.

Then when the exorcisms were performed and everyone who remembered where the body had been found had been moved away or fired, he brought a new crew to the old site.

And if there were men who still thought they saw on occasion a young naked woman running in the shadows of the cranes, peeking from behind a stack of concrete blocks, darting between steel girders, and once floating from floor to floor, he made sure the foreman tracked down and fired the rumormongers.

Workers who had time to gossip and indulge in storytelling were lazy and had no place in the new economy. Zhang had not been born yesterday. He understood well the price of doing business in the city these days.

CANADA

A FULL TWO MONTHS before the start of junior high, while I was still on Nancy Drew Number 46, *The Invisible Intruder* and the summer days stretched taffy slow from one Good Humor truck to the next, my best friend Maria Glinbizzi's mother drove her to the Willowbrook Mall to buy her first bra. Maria showed it to me when I went over to her house to play. She pulled it out of her dresser, wrapped in tissue in the plastic bag, tags still attached. It was white and stretchy and had two pink rosebuds sewn in the middle between the cups.

"Did you get yours yet?" Maria asked.

I felt my cheeks grow hot, and I looked down so my hair fell in front of my face, like looking at the bra was so interesting, I just couldn't look up again. "My mother says we're going to wait till the end of the summer."

"That's in case you grow," Maria said. "That's what my mother was worried about, too. But my dad said she'd better hurry up. Can you believe it? I can't believe my dad said that. At the dinner table. In front of Sean."

"Oh my god. I can't believe your dad said that." I was suddenly thankful my father was too busy ever to notice anything I was doing.

"I know," she said. Maria twisted one of her long, dark curly locks around her index finger. "That's why I'm hiding it. I think Sean and his stupid friends were looking through my stuff."

"What a jerk," I said.

"He's a pervert," Maria agreed.

Maria's brother was only a year behind us in school. Sometimes I'd see Sean in the hallway, waiting with his friends to go to the bathroom or lining up in front of the drinking fountain. At Maria's house, he was a like a little kid, sitting in front of the TV, shooting a toy gun at the Klingons, *pew pew pew!* But at school, the boys he hung out with whistled in the halls and called girls names.

I was glad my brother Charlie was three years younger. It made him more manageable.

At least when we started junior high in September, Sean would still be in elementary school, and we wouldn't have to worry about him for a year.

"Look, Lu-lu, do you wanna guess where it was made?" Maria took her bra back and pulled the tag up so that I could see. Very clearly in red letters it said, "Made in R.O.C." And suddenly my face burned anew. Republic of China. I knew exactly where that was on the map, a small island in the sea next to the bigger mainland. I thought of my grandparents who'd lived in Taipei before coming to America, Ye-ye, who always dressed up in his suit when we went out to eat for dinner as a family, and Nai-nai, who still wore her Chinese-style dresses in America. Still, the image came to me of dozens of old women who looked just like my grandmother hunched over sewing machines sewing little bras for American girls. I felt ashamed although I didn't know why. I braced myself for whatever Maria would say.

"*Rock*," she pronounced. "Isn't that funny? What kind of country is that?"

Poor Maria, I thought, relieved. But then I realized maybe this was secretly why we were friends. I could feel safe with her, always one step slightly ahead.

"Yeah," I said. "It's like *Rocky*, the movie." I laughed. "Yo, Adrian!" I called in my best Rocky voice.

"Yeah, yeah, it's just like that," and she snatched the bra back and put it over her shirt, her fists in the cups. "Yo, Adrian!" she called to herself and then pranced around, maybe she was supposed to be Adrian, or just some woman with a bra, something ridiculous like that, and we both laughed and laughed until Maria farted and then she turned red and ran outside her room, then back inside, and farted again. We both rolled on her carpet, hysterical.

I REMEMBER my mother originally hadn't been too keen on the idea of buying me a bra at all that summer. Mama said she was too busy to go shopping for school clothes yet. She was teaching night classes and was gone most evenings. On the weekends, she had papers to grade or "committee meetings." Besides, she added, "I didn't need a bra until I was thirteen." I wanted to add that she hadn't grown up in America, but in Canada, far away. Who knew what was normal there? Fortunately, the handouts from orientation for junior high were insistent: *Normative Underwear Required* was printed in bold on the list of things we had to buy before we started in the fall, like our gym shorts and t-shirts in school colors, appropriate footwear (no heels, no black soles that would scuff the gym floors), book covers, No. 2 pencils, and three-ring binders *With No Imagery On The Cover*. I'd pointed this out to Mama, and she glanced at the sheet and said, "Oh, bother."

Mama later handed me the Sears catalog with the corner turned down on the page for training bras. There were three varieties, all of them white as a starched nurse's uniform. One had a tiny pink-and-blue tennis racket between the cups, one had a white rosette,

and one was plain. Mama was going to order one from the catalog, but then she said, "You're probably going to need to try it on
first." And she'd sighed, in an aggrieved, angry manner, as though
I were becoming one more burden she had to deal with in the day.
You'd have thought it was like the time my cousin Madison got
ringworm and Aunt Mei had to sterilize all their towels. Mama's
voice sounded like I had caught something contagious. I didn't tell
any of that to Maria, though.

I hadn't thought much about bras up till this point. My chest was
flat and straight, and my belly was round and smooth and pressed
against my shirts still. I wondered if my lack of breasts might be
due to the fact that I was Chinese, but I had no other Chinese classmates, nothing to compare myself to except my mother, who always seemed perfect in her womanhood, the opposite of me. I had
no metric by which to tell what was normal.

But when I talked to Cindy Van Lenten, I noticed she was even
thinner than I was and six months older, which gave me some relief. I asked her straight up if she was going to try to do without,
but Cindy shook her head gravely. It was too risky, she said. If you
didn't wear a training bra in gym class, for example, and your boobs
started to come in, they could grow crooked and they'd be two
different sizes. They would never be normative when you grew
up, she said, unless your training bra was there to press them into
place. That's what the orientation packet meant. They hadn't fully
explained because they didn't want to scare us.

I nodded because that seemed right. Adults were just like that.
They only ever said half of what they meant.

LATER MAMA told Aunt Mei about my needing a training bra. I
couldn't believe my ears, the way she just blurted it out. I would have
thought having gone through this herself when she was young,

my mother would have had some sensitivity, but adults were always disappointing me.

It was late in the summer, Mama's night classes finally over, and so we'd gone to pick up Madison to play at our house, but Madison was still at her swimming lesson. Aunt Mei let us in to wait. She said the twins were sleeping finally. We all sat down in the living room, Mama on the piano bench and me on the armchair and Aunt Mei on the rocker. There were laundry baskets on the sofa and a diaper pail in the corner, and for the first time, the house didn't smell like Madison's rabbit.

"I was just soaking myself," Aunt Mei said. Then she unbuttoned her blouse, and I got to see her nursing bra, bright white and thick with snaps and triangular flaps that exposed the nipples, which were swollen and purply red, the areolas dark as bruises. She put a wet, cold Lipton teabag over each nipple, sighing. "Old wives trick, my mom used to say." She laughed, a short bark, like a seal. Then she closed her eyes and leaned her head against the afghan draped over the back of the rocking chair.

"I bottle-fed Lu-lu," Mama volunteered. "I wanted to breastfeed her, but I was under a lot of stress. I lost all my milk." (I kept waiting for her to add, "And she turned out all right," as she did at home, when she'd told my brother and me this story.) "But when Charlie came along, I was able to breastfeed a full six months. And he had quite the appetite."

"My mother breastfed me until I was almost four years old," Aunt Mei said with her eyes closed. She rocked back and forth, back and forth.

"Oh, is that so?"

"Mom was old school. Everything had to be the way her mother had done things. And Po-po was a tyrant. I remember growing up Mom and me had to scrub the floors on our hands and knees. Po-po said it was the only way to really get the dirt. She lived to be ninety-seven if you can believe it. Outlived Mom by five years."

"Did I meet your grandmother at the wedding?"

"That was her in the wheelchair with the oxygen tank." Aunt Mei let out another seal bark laugh. "I don't think she knew who I was anymore. Kept calling me by my Mom's name. Really, she took care of me more than my mother. She lived with us the whole time I was growing up so Mom could work."

"When did your father die?"

"Dad died of a heart attack before I was born."

"That's right. It must have been hard on your mother."

"I always blamed everything on his dying. If I'd grown up with a father figure. A father, I mean. If I'd gotten used to having a man in the house. Maybe I'd understand them better."

"No," Mom said. "Nothing prepares you. Nothing helps."

Aunt Mei looked as though she were asleep, slumped as she was into the rocking chair, but her right hand was moving, patting at the teabags on her nipples, adjusting them, prodding them, her fingers fluttering over her pendulous, milky breasts like nervous, flesh-colored moths while the rest of her body just lay there, dead.

I looked away quickly, held my book before my nose, but I couldn't focus on the words on the page. Seeing Aunt Mei prone and lifeless made me nervous, made my heart beat too fast. I wasn't sure who I could share this story with, not Charlie, he was a boy, and not Madison, who was too young, but it didn't seem like something Cindy Van Lenten or Maria Glinbizzi would appreciate. We had the usual things we talked about, TV shows and movies and books and other kids at school and weird things teachers had said or done when they thought we weren't looking. I couldn't see how to bring in such a separate, adult experience.

Madison's pet bunny hopped cautiously past the living room

door and slipped behind the sofa. I saw the curtains rustle and knew it was moving deeper and deeper into hiding where it could chew on power cords and the underpart of the couch undisturbed. I knew because Madison had told me about her parents' fights, how her mother had threatened to get rid of it after coming home and finding a giant hole in the middle of a cushion, white stuffing like snowflakes spread about the carpet.

"We're going to buy Lu-lu a training bra this summer," Mama told Aunt Mei.

All the heat in my body rushed to my face. I looked daggers at my mother, but she was folding the laundry from one of the baskets, smoothing washcloths against the arm of the sofa.

"Time flies," Aunt Mei said.

I used to like to eavesdrop every opportunity, gathering their secrets like breadcrumbs that would lead me from a dark forest someday, but lately they didn't even try to hide their problems from me. They spoke in front of me as though they thought I should care. Aunt Mei had even told the nurses in the hospital it was okay for me to come up and visit her after the twins were born. Technically, I was too young, only eleven, the hospital had a sign that said visitors had to be twelve or older. But Aunt Mei insisted and told the nurses I was twelve. "Let Lu-lu see her cousins," she'd said. Charlie had had to wait downstairs, but the nurses had led me to a long glass window and pointed out the incubators where the twins lay inside.

"Can you see 'em?" The nurse smiled and tapped on the window, pointing, as though we were in a pet store staring at puppies through the glass. But puppies were cute.

I'd nodded then, solemnly, although all I could see was light reflecting off all that glass and plastic and metal.

When I came back down the elevator, Charlie was sitting in the molded plastic seats of the lobby reading a comic book.

"I saw them," I announced.

He looked up.

"They look like sea monkeys," I said. It wasn't fair that Charlie was allowed to be oblivious and happy. I pointed to the picture of the horned, smiling anthropomorphized brine shrimp drawn on the back of his Fantastic Four comic. "They're really ugly."

Charlie nodded and turned back to the comic. "That's what Uncle Roger said."

FINALLY, UNCLE Roger and Madison came back from the Y. I could hear the car pull up into the driveway. Madison came running inside, her towel over her shoulder. Her damp hair lay slick against her head, making her look even more doll-like than usual.

"Don't wake the babies," Aunt Mei hissed, and Madison stopped in her tracks.

But one of the twins woke up. A tinny shriek echoed from their bedroom.

"Come on, Madison," Uncle Roger said from the door. He held the screen open for her. "Don't bother your mother." And Madison ran out again.

Aunt Mei got up and came back with a twin on each forearm. She brought one over to me.

"Don't you want to hold her," she said, and I knew I wasn't allowed to say no.

The baby was small but grew heavy against my arm when no one took it back. I was afraid I'd hurt it, so much more fragile than a plastic doll, though about the same size. I looked into the tight balled-fist of its face, watched it open and close its lipless mouth. It wasn't as pretty as a baby doll either.

I had to sit very still on the sofa, my arms growing stiff from the weight of the baby. Uncle Roger was helping Madison catch fireflies on the lawn. I could hear their laughter through the window.

Mama and Aunt Mei talked and talked. Who knew they could be so interested in the amount of poop the twins were now depositing into their diapers, the color and consistency and smell? They used to talk about Uncle Roger and Papa ("The Lin Boys," as Aunt Mei called them), comparing their temperaments, gauging their emotions. Sometimes they talked about their own families who lived far away, comparing the problems of cousins I'd never met but whose names were familiar only in relation to stories set in the long-ago times before my mother and Aunt Mei were married. "I married too quickly," Mama said once. "I just wanted to get away from my family. I'm too impetuous."

"You? You're a rock," Aunt Mei said, then laughed.

"Oh, don't call me that," Mama said.

"But it's true! *My* rock!"

LAST YEAR when Aunt Mei and Uncle Roger were going through their "difficulties" and Uncle Roger spent more and more time at work and didn't come home at all one weekend, Aunt Mei had brought Madison over to our house and sat in the dining room with Mama, crying. Mama told me to keep Madison entertained, so we were allowed to let our Siberian Husky, George, inside the family room, and we played Star Wars. We strapped a plastic bandolier across George's back so he could be Chewbacca, which meant Charlie was Han Solo. There was only one girl in Star Wars, but I let Madison play Princess Leia since her mother was the one crying, which made me feel generous. That meant I had to be C-3Po, but that was okay, because in my version, he was smart and bossy and everyone else listened when he told them what to do.

We'd escaped the trash compactor three times and were en route to blow up the Death Star the second time around before Aunt Mei was finally ready to take Madison home. We were sitting on the couch cushions on the floor in X-Wing formations, brandishing paper-towel-roll light sabers. When we turned around, Aunt Mei was standing in the doorway, arms folded across her chest watching us. She wasn't crying anymore, but she wasn't smiling either. She was staring at us playing.

Mama called through the door, "Hurry up and finish. Madison has to go home." And we charged Darth Vader and killed him and then blew up the new Death Star in our wake as we fled, running back and forth across the linoleum. George's paws kept sliding, and he plowed into us, then howled.

We all laughed, even Mama.

"Come on. Playtime's over," Aunt Mei said, her voice flat.

Madison gave me back her light saber. "Mommy, George was Chewbacca," she said.

But Aunt Mei wasn't standing in the doorway watching us anymore. She'd already left.

THE TWIN in my arms raised a fist and punched its own eye. I thought it would've cried and braced myself, my whole body tensing, but instead the baby merely twisted its face into a surprised knot and tried inserting its fist into its mouth.

"Do you want the baby back?" I suggested hopefully.

"You can keep holding her," Aunt Mei said. Her eyes were half-closed, as she leaned back in the rocker, pushing her feet against the floor so the rocker creaked back and forth, *crik-crik, crik-crik*. "It's okay," she said.

"I think she's hungry," I said.

I was hoping Mama would notice that I'd been holding that baby for a very long time now and wanted to go and play, but Mama didn't say anything. She picked up the other twin and rocked it in her arms. "Aren't they precious? Aren't they just like little dolls at this age? I almost wanted a third child, but Walter felt two were enough."

"Two is a hell of a lot," Aunt Mei said.

"Walter always gets his way," Mama said. "He pretends to be very easy-going, but in fact he's the opposite. Extremely stubborn. A workaholic. We never do anything anymore. We never go to the city. If there's one thing I've learned about marriage—"

At that moment, Madison came in the front door, her hands cupped together, holding a firefly. Madison, secretive as her bunny, her black eyes taking in everything and revealing nothing, tossed the bug into the air. It circled through the room dizzily, up and down, but I couldn't see its light blink. In the yellow glow of the living room lamps it just seemed like an ordinary insect.

"Madison, cut it out!" Aunt Mei barked. "What did I say about no horsing around?"

Madison turned on her heels and fled. The screen door slammed shut behind her, and the baby in my arms erupted into a long, piercing wail.

Aunt Mei and Mama turned to stare at me, their eyes fixed on me as if they'd only then remembered I was in the room. I thought they were going to yell at me, but then Aunt Mei burst into laughter. Not her seal-bark laugh but a new sound, a laugh that honked through her nose. Then Mama laughed, covering her mouth as though she were coughing. She bent at the waist and put her hand on Aunt Mei's arm, and Aunt Mei's face turned bright red from the effort as she honked-honked-honked through her nose and Mama wheezed another laugh into her hand like a sneeze.

"What's so funny?" I asked. I couldn't help but smile, they were laughing so much, but for the life of me I couldn't figure out why on earth they were laughing at me.

I REMEMBER we didn't actually get my bra until it was almost time for school, just two weeks to go, and we'd already picked up Charlie's supplies from the A&P, the crayons and glue and blunt-tipped scissors they still required in elementary school although Charlie had been allowed to use regular scissors and even an X-Acto knife at home for years. But finally, one Saturday, Mama acted as though she suddenly remembered something she'd been forgetting and told Papa to watch Charlie. "Girls' shopping day," she said, and blessedly he didn't ask any questions.

The training bras at Stern's were hidden in the back behind the women's slips and the silky pajamas, far enough away from the regular brassieres so as not to be intimidating. That was a relief. To see them hanging discretely on a divider between the lingerie and hosiery sections.

The light shone from above so the white polyester looked even whiter than usual, like an advertisement for bleach, and I said, loudly, "Oh, look at the bathrobes" and pointed past the bras to the tangled rack of robes, just in case anyone was watching us, just to throw them.

Mama walked right up to them, though. She scanned the rows and plucked one from the hanger. Then she held it up to my body to check the size, pressing the fabric against my blouse, against the flatness of my chest, right there in the aisle for the whole world to see.

"Oh my god! Mama!" I exclaimed, and, dying, I slipped away into hosiery, disappearing into the displays of upturned plaster legs kicking into the air. My heart was pounding, my cheeks burning, and my eyes stung. I blinked and blinked again. All around me were picture after picture of women with their arms crossed over their naked torsos, lounging in nothing but pantyhose over their long legs in taupe, suntan, nude, and shimmer. It seemed they were deliberately mocking me as I crouched near the floor in shame, pretending to tie my shoelaces.

Fortunately, Mama didn't come looking for me. Or worse, call my name.

I watched from my hiding spot as she found a saleslady to ring up the bra.

I crouched down again and hid, watching Mama walk away with a silver and black Stern's bag under her arm. After a pause, I was going to come out again, wander over nonchalantly holding a package of tights, but there weren't any for girls. I was in the wrong section entirely, I discovered, when I heard Mama's voice rising in laughter.

I hoped none of my friends' mothers were here. I didn't want anyone to find out about this until I'd had time to tell them myself. Humiliation was easier to control that way.

But the next voice wasn't a woman's. It was low and rumbly. A man.

What crazy father would be here in the women's section? I thought. Seriously, not even Mr. Glinbizzi would do that. That's why there were chairs by the elevators. Men waited there for their wives and talked to each other. I'd seen them.

I followed the sound of Mama's voice and found her in the aisle, my Stern's bag still under her arm. She was laughing at something that man was saying. He was wearing a suit jacket, tweed; I knew because Papa had one like that too. But this man was older, with gray in his curly hair, and he was white.

"Linda," he said, and the way he said it made Mama laugh again.

I hurried over. "Hey, Mom," I said, my voice a little too loud in my own ears. "They didn't have any tights in my size." And I bumped into her arm.

"And this must be Lu-lu," the man said.

I didn't like that he knew my name.

"That's not how you're supposed to say it," I said. "It's Chinese. It has tones. *Lu. Lu.*" I tried to pronounce it just like Ye-ye and Nai-nai did, loud.

"Oh, Lu-lu," Mama said, the way she always did, but the man laughed, so Mama laughed, too.

"Well, it was very nice running into you, Linda," he said.

"Likewise," Mama said. She tucked a strand of her hair behind her ear as she spoke. "Lu-lu, Tom is a colleague from work. He teaches in the extension program."

Tom, I thought.

"I'll work on those tones," the man said. "LU LU."

I smiled in a tight way, the way Maria and Cindy and I did when we were being fake polite to girls we didn't like in school, but this man didn't seem to notice.

"She's just beautiful," he said to Mama.

And Mama said, "Thank you," as though she'd been the one he was complimenting.

Even though Mama didn't say anything more, I was in a sour mood the whole drive back home.

I couldn't even look forward to calling Cindy and Maria and telling them about my bra. What could I say?

THAT NIGHT at dinner Mama was particularly happy. Papa said her spaghetti was delicious, and Charlie asked if he could get another dog. He'd been reading about Bassett Hounds in school and he would like a Bassett Hound.

Papa said, "Absolutely not."

Mama said, "Honey, George will resent another dog."

"I think we should get another dog," I said. The words just fell out of my mouth, surprising me.

Papa and Mama turned to stare. They weren't used to my taking Charlie's side in anything.

"A Bassett Hound would be nice," I said. "It could be my dog. I don't have a dog."

"But, Lu-lu, you'll be too busy. You're starting school in two weeks. And junior high is very different from elementary school," Mama said. She smiled then, but not a nice one. She said, "Lu-lu and I went shopping for junior high today."

And I knew then she was going to mention the training bra. I wouldn't have thought it possible, the betrayal from my own mother, but she had the same look in her eye that teachers got when they were going to spring a pop quiz, the look that meant business.

"You're right," I said. "I'm going to be too busy. Besides, George will feel bad."

"But, Maaa—" Charlie started, drawing his voice into a whine.

"Listen to Lu-lu!" Papa said, saying my name in tones. "Your sister's older. She knows what she's talking about."

Charlie dropped his chin into his chest. "It's not fair!" Then he pushed back his chair noisily and ran up the stairs.

Papa sighed and continued eating, and Mama turned to me and wrinkled her nose. I knew that was how she winked, her own special version to compensate because she couldn't quite close only one eyelid at a time. She used to do this when I was younger and she took me to get ice cream on Saturday mornings after grocery shopping, just the two of us, while Charlie was at home watching cartoons and Papa worked in his study. "Girls have to have their secrets," she'd say, wrinkling her nose.

And automatically, I winked back at her, first my left eye, then my right, because that was how I'd practiced in the mirror, over and over till I'd gotten it down.

But this night, I didn't feel happy winking with my mother. Who ever said I'd wanted to have secrets? Whose big idea was that?

There was nothing I could do, however. Secrets were better than telling the embarrassing truth. A girl didn't need to be in junior high to know that.

THAT NIGHT long after my family had gone to bed, I lay in my bed reading. I had two books hidden under my pillows—a Trixie Belden mystery and a new Nancy Drew—and a third tucked between the mattress and the wall that I could pull out as soon as the lights went out in my parents' room and I knew Mama wasn't going to come back in and tell me to turn off the light. I also kept a flashlight on my dresser for times when Mama stayed up very late and insisted, "Lights out, Lu-lu!" in the voice that meant business. Sometimes I was too absorbed in my reading and she came in to check on me before I could turn off the light and pretend to be asleep. Then she'd say, "You're ruining your eyes! Turn that light off and go to sleep!" I'd told her the eye doctor said that wasn't true. Reading had nothing to do with ruining my eyes. He'd told me he would've been able to predict I'd need glasses if he'd been able to peer into my irises when I was first born, but Mama didn't believe it.

But she was sound asleep and hadn't come creeping through the hall since she went to bed.

This night none of my books could occupy me. I read a few pages in one, part of a chapter in another, but I could not enter the stories and live with the characters as usual. The world outside my books seemed suddenly too noisy. I could hear the faucet dripping in the bathroom and water running through the pipes in the wall. The wind was not particularly strong, but I could hear the maple trees swaying. A few leaves had already started to turn, the yellow seeping into the green along the top branches, and now I could hear the crisper leaves take flight, crackling like fire as they fell.

Outside George was shaking his head and jangling the tags on his collar. He yawned and stretched and I heard his toenails click against the cement floor of the patio, and then he was off, launched, running through the yard, chasing something in the night.

I lay in bed waiting. He ran round and round, his feet thundering against the grass, and then he stopped abruptly to shake his head and yawn. I could hear his tags as he circled, chasing his tail, before plopping back down.

Summer was coming to an end. George didn't run like that when it was hot. He lay on his side, panting, twitching his tall, stiff ears to keep the flies away, drool running off his tongue. He only liked to run when the weather was cooler.

Finally, I got up to get a glass of water. And while I was standing in the bathroom, Dixie cup in hand staring at my reflection in the mirror, I realized this would be a perfect time to try it on, my bra, while everyone was still asleep. I tiptoed back to my room and pulled the Stern's bag back from under my dresser where I'd hidden it. Carefully peeling apart the crackly paper bag as quietly as possible, I pulled the bright-white bra from within, rumpled it tightly in my fist, and then brought it under my pajama top, as though the whiteness would show through like moonlight or the rays of a tractor beam. I ran back to the bathroom and locked the door.

I pulled my shirt up and slipped my arms through the loops then I had to hook it from behind, which was harder than I'd thought. I had to bend over at the waist, my elbows bowed out like wings, till I could slide the hook into the eye.

Then I turned and faced the mirror.

The training bra was white as chalk against my skin, like crime scene outlines across my chest where a bosom was supposed to appear, or worse, had been murdered and taken away. My breath caught in my throat and for a second I wondered if something really was wrong with me. Why did my nipples seem to be so low? Why did my belly protrude from beneath my rib cage, round like a baby's? With the bra strapped in place, I could suddenly see what my body was supposed to look like, like women on magazine covers in bikinis or Jane Russell crossing her heart on TV, and I was nothing like them. I was lumpen and doughy, but not in the outlined areas. Before the bra, I had never even imagined I was supposed to resemble them, but now I felt profoundly inadequate.

I pulled my pajama top back on over my head, hoping that maybe the bra looked better under clothes, but the effect was even worse. The soft cotton t-shirt no longer lay flat against my skin. Instead the outlines of the bra showed through, disturbing the lines of the picture of Princess Leia cradling her blaster on the front. I'd seen girls like this, teenagers whose bras showed through their t-shirts so that you couldn't focus on the picture or saying in front, all you could notice was the bra. I'd always felt sorry for them. Now here I was. The same.

Then I heard the noise from downstairs. A rustling. Not a breaking or a smashing, but a soft sound, like the time George had gotten out of the family room where Mama had put him during a storm, and we'd returned from school to find him lying on the living room carpet methodically chewing on Charlie's sneakers.

I held my breath and listened. I couldn't hear George running outside anymore, only the wind.

It didn't seem possible he could have gotten in, but I thought I should check. I tiptoed down the hall and paused at the top of the stairs, listening. Then I stepped onto the first stair, adjusting my

weight slowly so that it wouldn't creak. Just in case it wasn't George
but someone else. I wasn't stupid. I knew how to be very quiet. This
was how I'd discovered Mama and Papa putting the presents under
the tree instead of Santa Claus when I was five, unlike Charlie who
bounded about wherever he went. You had plenty of time to hide
things before he arrived.

I crept down one stair at a time, stealthy as a real detective, and
when I reached the bottom, I crouched and peered around the corner, but George wasn't in the living room. It was Papa stretched out
on the sofa, asleep.

I stood up.

He shouldn't have been there. He only slept on the sofa when he
came home from work late and didn't want to disturb us by creak-
ing up the stairs. I know, because he used to do that. Come home
late and wake us up, but Mama got angry. She told him that was
very inconsiderate. He knew how much trouble she had getting
Charlie to settle down in the first place, and now Charlie would
have trouble getting up in the morning for school. After that, Papa
said he was sorry, and he promised to sleep on the couch the next
time he was late.

But he hadn't come home late. And here he was all the same.

I tiptoed to the middle of the living room so that I could see him
better, past the piano and right up to the coffee table with the picture books of *Great Works of Art* and *Treasures of the Natural World*
from *National Geographic* and the empty cloisonné bowl that was
just for decoration.

His face was slack, his mouth turned down, and his eyes puffy-
looking without their glasses over them. He lay very still. I held my
breath, suddenly thinking something terrible, something terrify-
ing, but then he breathed out, very slowly, his chest falling from
under the chenille throw that was supposed to be in the family

room. I wanted to wake him up immediately, the way I had when I was a little girl and I needed something right away. One year I'd gotten up at dawn for Christmas, but Mama said we couldn't open any presents until everyone was awake. Papa slept late on holidays, and by mid-morning I couldn't stand the wait. I filled a glass with cold water from the kitchen and brought it to the bedroom and poured it on his face.

He hadn't been angry.

But I didn't dare do that now. I wasn't a little girl anymore, I couldn't pretend I didn't know better.

I crept back to the edge of the staircase and sat on the bottom, my knees bent against my chest, my head against my arms, the tags on my bra scratching at my skin. I didn't even have a book to pass the time, but it didn't matter. The answer I needed wasn't in a book. Instead I sensed that I should sit, I should be patient, I should wait like this until my father finally woke up.

THE LUCKY DAY

'M AWAKE. YOU don't have to sneak around." Ma's voice drifted like smoke from beneath the covers.

"Ma, it's April twelfth." Rose spoke in Chinese to her mother, but that meant there were things she couldn't explain, like how she had hoped things would be different between them this time, how she hoped Ma would be pleased by this visit, would see her for the kind and thoughtful daughter she was.

She'd driven from Colorado to Iowa through the night, eight hours, despite the snow pack on the interstate, just to see Ma for her birthday. But now Ma didn't even seem surprised to see Rose.

"I know what day it is. Why are you standing in the dark?"

Rose set the pink box of lucky dried fruit on the end table, pushing the pill bottles to the side. Her mother's room smelled like overripe bananas.

"I'll open the curtains. There was a snowstorm last night, Ma. *A real blizzard,*" she added in English for emphasis. "Wanna see?" Blue-white light flooded into the room.

Ma shielded her eyes with one hand. "Well, this killed the flowers. There was a crocus and three yellow daffodils right by the driveway. I could see them from the window. Dead now."

"There'll be more."

"Not for me."

"Don't say that."

"Why not? Look at me."

"You look good," Rose lied.

"I look like a skinned rat. I look like something your grandfather would have eaten. I look like an ugly old woman." Ma put her face in her hands.

"Where's your hair?" Rose didn't know how to say "wig" in Chinese, but her mother understood.

"I don't know."

Rose searched in the dresser and the closet shelf and under the bed and finally, patting around Ma's covers, found it buried under the blankets along with a pair of wool socks. It was a dark brown bob with curls, nothing like Ma's real hair.

Ma set the wig atop her skull, adjusting it by feel, twisting it this way and that. She patted it with one hand.

"How does that look?"

"A little bit more to the right. There. That's perfect."

Suddenly Marisol poked her head in the door.

"Good morning, Sleepyhead! Did you have a good rest last night?" Rose's sister-in-law spoke in the bright metallic English of a host for a children's television show.

Ma winced.

"*Make her go away,*" she hissed in English, loud enough for Rose's sister-in-law to hear.

"Better try to eat your breakfast today. You know what the doctor said. We don't want to be a bad girl now, do we?"

Ma put her hands over her ears, shut her eyes tight.

"Do what you can, Rose. She's been cranky wanky like this for weeks." Marisol dropped the smile and disappeared, shutting the door behind her with a sharp click.

Rose tapped her mother's arm. "She's gone."

"I need my eyebrows." Ma waved a hand at the shoeboxes.

Rose dug around until she found Ma's Mary Kay compact and eyeliner in a box marked VITAMINS but filled with empty pill bottles.

"Here, Ma."

Ma pursed her lips and turned her head from side to side, examining herself in the tiny mirror.

"Well." She sighed. The mirror cast diamonds across her cheekbones. "I used to be good-looking. I turned a lot of heads in my day. I was really something."

"Drink a little Ensure, Ma. It has vitamins."

"I don't like Ensure. But put a little of the morphine in my Hawaiian Punch. There's a dropper. Count the drops. I'll tell you when."

Rose found Ma's cup of juice with a bendy straw in it and the bottle of Roxanol. "One, two, three . . . four?"

"Good enough." Ma took the cup, fitted the straw between her lips and sucked. She handed the cup back to Rose. "And I need a cigarette."

"I don't—"

"Yes, you do. I can smell the smoke. They stole all my cigarettes." Ma nodded at the door. "Even the pack I hid in the closet. That's how I know *that woman* spies on me."

"Okay." Rose tried to remember where she'd left her gym bag. When she'd arrived at dawn, she was both exhausted from the drive and still hopped up from Mountain Dew and nicotine. She tiptoed out into the hallway, found her bag by the front door with her sneakers. Sam and Marisol were whispering in the kitchen. Rose walked past the open door twice. The whispering never stopped.

Rose lit a cigarette for Ma then one for herself. The last two in her pack.

Ma inhaled deeply. She barely coughed at all and managed to exhale a large ring of smoke like a halo. "You see, perfect," Ma said, triumph in her voice.

"They'll smell the smoke. Maybe I should light some of the incense on the shrine." Rose got up and checked around the dresser top. She finally found a cone—*Night Jasmine*—in a red ashtray. She lit it with her Zippo. Out of habit, she bowed her head quickly, three times before the framed picture of the Buddha.

Then she sat back down on the bed. They stayed like that, side by side, without talking, until Ma dunked her cigarette into her cup of morphine-spiked fruit punch.

She exhaled two streams of blue smoke from her nostrils.

"There's no hope for us. I can't see how we're going to survive in this world. I saw your bruises."

"I'm fine. I fell." Rose didn't want to argue with Ma about her life again. Some days it seemed all she did was argue with people. Customers at the coffee shop. The kids she tutored on weekends. Their parents. But no, not everyone. Rose had made the police officer smile from the back of the squad car. The neighbors were still screaming, and she was spotting blood, but she told him jokes until he cracked a smile. "Sunshine, don't let nobody put a cloud over that face of yours. You got the light in you," he'd said.

Tell that to my asshole boyfriend, Rose had thought but not said. Instead she'd smiled. Rose had learned cops were easier to control when she smiled.

"You don't know how to manage in this life," Ma continued, ticking off Rose's many failures: she hadn't finished her degree, she had every opportunity that Ma had not but still no profession, no marriage.

"I'm going back to school soon. I just needed to take a break." Rose wasn't lying exactly.

The door opened and Sam stuck his head inside. He kept his hair cut short, like he was still in the Marines. All the baby fat was gone now, his cheekbones seemed chiseled from a warm, smooth stone. But he was still wide-eyed, just as he had been as a child, alert, observing everything.

He sniffed.

"You can't smoke around Mom!" He scowled.

"Sammy, you look so tired. You should not work so hard." Ma switched to English, just for her son.

Sam could have been all of eight years old again in Ma's presence.

"Mommy! Can I get you anything? I'm heading to work."

"When did you get so polite, Squirt?" Rose smirked, but her younger brother ignored her.

"You change the fruit? I dreamed about your father last night," Ma said.

"We put up a new bowl yesterday."

"That wife of yours, she didn't throw them away?"

"Marisol even picked some flowers for the vase. I bought some oranges and apples and a banana."

"All the praying she does to God, I don't know what she wants."

"Mom, she wants you to get better."

"She makes me pray *a rosary* every night," Ma stage-whispered to Rose.

"It's for your health." Sam's voice trembled. "God can still cure you."

"My sister used to do that, too. Before she died. Didn't do any good. All those Catholic prayers."

"Ma, do you want Sam to get anything before he goes to work?" Rose asked quickly. She didn't drive all night and lose so much sleep just to play referee in a fight over religion.

"You look tired, Sammy." Ma patted his head, smoothed his hair. "You let that wife of yours do some work. When I first married, I worked all the time."

"Did you remember, Sam? It's Ma's birthday." Rose was sure her brother had forgotten.

"At my age, what do I care about my birthday," Ma said.

"I'm sorry. I forgot. Happy birthday!" Sam noticed her cup. "Do you need some more juice?"

"No, no, no. Rose is here. She can help me. You rest. You work too hard."

Sam sniffed, on the verge of breaking down. He bent close to Ma, and she wrapped her arms around his muscular shoulders and patted him on the back. "You're my good boy," she said. Sam sniffed again and turned away so Rose wouldn't see him tear up.

"This year will be better, Mom. I know it." Sam looked as earnest as he had as a boy bringing home his report card for his mother's approval.

"Of course it will. The horoscope book says it will be my best year ever."

Sam nodded and headed out the door. Then he turned back toward Rose. "Don't wear Mommy out with all your talking, Rose."

"Shut up, Squirt."

Sam flipped Rose the bird cheerfully and headed out, shutting the door softly behind him.

Ma waited until she heard his car pull out of the driveway. "Pick me up," Ma demanded. "I would like a shower."

"Are you sure it's a good idea?"

"It's my birthday. I deserve to be clean. You can help me."

Ma wrapped her arms around Rose's neck. Rose could almost count Ma's ribs through her sweater.

They walked to the bathroom in tiny steps. When Rose was a teenager, the house had seemed so small compared to houses on TV, she'd felt her siblings' presence in every room, Lily and Daisy and Sam suffocating her, but now the hallway seemed to stretch, her mother leaning on her heavily, each step a struggle.

When they got to the bathroom, Rose was sweating slightly, but Ma was in good spirits. "Now get the water ready," she commanded. "It's been so long since I had a good shower. *That woman wants me to take a sponge bath!*"

Rose set her mother gently on the toilet seat then bent over the tub, adjusting the water. When she turned around again, she was startled to find Ma, normally so modest, completely naked, smiling like a mischievous child, her cotton pajamas and panties and wig lying in a heap at her feet.

"I'm ready," Ma announced.

Rose helped Ma into the tub, leaned her against the tile wall, then sprayed her with the removable shower nozzle.

Ma closed her eyes. "Over here," she directed, pointing. "No, there." She rubbed her hands in the warm water and splashed it over her bald head. She smiled.

"I'm the baby now," she said. "You're the mother!" She splashed water at Rose.

"Ma, stop it!" But Ma only laughed.

"It used to be the tradition to bathe for the new year. But that was long ago," Ma said, lifting one arm then the other so that Rose could spray the sides of her body. "Back in the village, we just had one tub of water for everyone in the family."

"Yuck."

Ma opened her eyes just to glare at Rose. "Careful. Don't get water in my face."

Rose put the plastic nozzle back on its metal hook and grabbed the white bar of Dove from its dish. She soaped Ma from her flat feet to her wide thighs, across the folds of her belly, underneath her saggy breasts, over the hard, raised bump where the port for the chemo lay beneath the skin, up and down her thin arms, which had once been ironed with muscles. She washed the wrinkles of Ma's neck and the whorls of her ears and the top of her smooth, round skull. And then gently, she cupped her hands beneath the shower nozzle and poured handful after handful of water over Ma's skin until the soap had been washed off completely and the water ran clear.

Finally, she gently wrapped Ma in two thick bath towels like a glass figurine that might break.

"I turned a few heads when I was a young girl," Ma said. She stroked the pale blue towel about her head as though the ends were plaits of long, shiny hair. "My sister had the prettier face, but I had a better figure. My breasts were round like melons, and my waist was so slender. It's a pity none of you girls looked more like me."

Rose helped Ma shuffle back through the hallway.

"Are you two girls all right?" Marisol emerged from the kitchen as though she sensed a conspiracy.

"Ma wanted a shower. For her birthday."

"I could have shown you, Rose. We have a bath chair for her." Marisol folded her arms across her chest.

"I'm fine, I'm fine." Ma shuffled faster into her room. She called behind her, "Go to work now. My daughter will take care of me."

Rose locked the bedroom door behind them.

Ma eased herself onto the edge of her bed as Rose searched for clean clothes in the dresser. There were balls and balls of socks, neatly folded t-shirts, but no underpants. "Do you know where Marisol puts your underwear?"

"We should commit suicide together."

"No, Ma. I can't do that." Ma and her dramatic pronouncements.

Rose remembered the way her parents used to argue, the shouting that made the walls shake, the deathly threats. She hadn't realized when she was a child that her parents' arguments were a sign of their verbal creativity, not actual violence. She hadn't recognized the difference in her ex until it was almost too late.

Rose felt tired. Driving all night had been a bad idea. Once upon a time, she had never needed to sleep. Work, school, party, and up again to start all over. But she hadn't been a teenager for a long time. Her smoking wasn't helping. Rose stretched her hands deep into the sock drawer and found a pair of pink nylon panties in the very back.

"Your next life might be better than this one," Ma said.

"Lift your left leg." Rose slipped Ma's foot through one side of her underpants. "Right leg." Rose pulled Ma's pants up over her hairless vagina, her protruding hipbones.

"That boyfriend of yours will never leave his wife. You're no longer young. What's the point of living?" Ma trembled.

"We broke up a long time ago." Rose buttoned up her mother's blouse. She held Ma's bony shoulders in her hands and felt her tremble.

Ma leaned against her pillows, perspiration beading across her brown forehead. "Open that Gatorade for me. It's time for my morphine."

Rose found a cleanish mug on the dresser since the old cup was filled with ashes. Rose poured in the Gatorade, added four drops of Roxanol, leaned the bendy straw at just the right angle. "Just the way you like it." Rose turned to the bed.

But Ma had nodded off.

She'd slid down so that only her tiny brown head appeared above the mound of pastel bath towels. Her face looked oddly at peace, as though she were a wealthy lady in an advertisement for a luxury spa.

Rose leaned close and checked for breathing until Ma's breath escaped in a slight snore.

Relieved, Rose lay down on the floor beside Ma's bed. She placed her hands over her belly, which rumbled angrily. She was hungry but not hungry enough to get up off the floor.

Before she knew it, Rose fell into a deep, untroubled sleep. When she was very little, Rose used to sleep beside her mother in the same bed. In those days the restaurant hadn't taken off and her father had to work a night shift at the John Deere plant in Waterloo to make ends meet.

Lying by her side, Ma would tell Rose stories about her life in the village before she was married, when she fought with her sister, the adventures the two girls had swimming in rivers, spying on monks, catching insects and snakes, when she'd never imagined what it would be like to live in another country and to have children of her own. Rose fell asleep to the sound of her mother's voice in her ear. Maybe this was the root of her insomnia, the silence that seemed to press around her in the dark when she was alone. Rose could never grow used to it.

Maybe this was the problem with how she chose men, the louder the better to fill the Ma-sized hole in her bed.

Ma woke first. She pushed at her tangle of sheets like a butterfly in a spider's web. She called out, and Rose sat up on the floor without even opening her eyes first. Her mother's voice had that effect on her.

"You have to help me. Quickly." Ma lifted her arms.

Rose jumped to her feet too fast, the room spinning around her, and she tumbled into the bed beside her mother. "No, no, no. Help me up," Ma said, annoyed, and Rose felt better. Her mother couldn't be dying, not anytime soon, if she could sound so irritable, so very normal.

Rose helped her mother out of bed. Ma leaned against the wall.

"Now pick up the mattress," Ma commanded.

"What?"

"Hurry! She could be coming any minute!"

Rose picked up the end of the mattress. Ma leaned forward so quickly that Rose gasped, thinking her mother was falling. But no, Ma was reaching underneath, patting around with her long, thin fingers.

"There!" she cried triumphantly. Ma waved a manila envelope in the air. "What are you waiting for? Put my bed down."

Rose set the mattress back atop the box springs and Ma sat down heavily, flipping through her envelope, thick and worn-looking and filled with cash. "You never know," Ma said, rifling through the bills. "Maybe she already found it and took some."

"Marisol wouldn't do that."

"You have no idea." Ma sat on the edge of the bed, licked a finger, and counted, flipping fives and twenties and the occasional hundred-dollar bill.

"You should have put that in the bank anyway." Rose found one of Ma's sweaters in the dresser and laid it over her thin shoulders.

"All here." Ma sighed. "Four thousand three hundred and fifty."

"Dollars?"

Ma rolled her eyes. "This is what I need you to do for me." She handed Rose the envelope. "Put this in your bag. So they don't find it."

For a second, Rose thought her mother was giving her the money. Rose's heart rose like salmon swimming upstream, flipped against the barrier of her ribcage. "I can't, Ma."

If I take her money, she will die, Rose thought.

"You aren't listening. Of course you can. I want you to drive me to Altoona." Ma buttoned up her cardigan matter-of-factly. "It's my lucky day. I can feel it. My horoscope said it's my lucky year. Well, there's nothing lucky about cancer, so there has to be something else."

Slowly, Rose found her voice. "You want to go to the track? It's freezing outside. There's a foot of snow!"

"I only ask this one thing, and my daughter refuses to help her old Ma." Ma pulled at the collar of her pink cardigan. "What kind of birthday is this?"

"It's not—I just don't want you to catch cold." If anything went wrong, it would be Rose's fault. What would Rose say to everyone then? "What about your white count?"

Ma wrinkled her wide, flat nose. "You sound like an old woman. White count, black count. I don't care what count. I want to bet on the horses."

"We can't leave," Rose said desperately. "Sam and Marisol will throw a fit. They'll be very worried."

"Sam is at work. He works in the restaurant every day. Never takes a day off. And that wife of his won't care what we do. Tell her you're taking me to the store. Or the hospital. She's waiting for me to die. I was a daughter-in-law, too. I remember what it was like." Ma turned to face Rose, her black eyes shining beneath her thin penciled-on brows.

"Ma, you really shouldn't go out in your condition. It's too dangerous. You could catch—"

"Aha! You do think I'm going to die!"

"No, Ma, it's just—"

"Well, you're right. I am going to die. I'm stage four. I know what *palliative* means. But I'm also going to bet on the horses." She sniffed, her lids fluttering rapidly. "Just in time for my birthday. We should celebrate. My daughter has come home to see me. Even the snow couldn't stop you. Not one of my other daughters could take the time. But you drive all this way. You see, it's my lucky day. I'm going to win. I can feel it."

Rose wondered how she could have forgotten about her mother's stubbornness, her charm, her manipulative nature, her moods like storms. Far from home, in Rose's memories, Ma had become like a black-and-white movie that she had watched on TV when she was a kid. Flickering and quaint. Up close in real life, Ma burned like a live coal against Rose's heart.

Rose slipped the manila envelope into the top of her jeans against her skin, pulled her Broncos sweatshirt down, and put her arm around her mother's back. "Okay, let's go," she said.

FIRST CARVEL IN BEIJING

T'S A LITTLE hole in the wall," Luce says, humble-bragging, "but they make the best dan dan noodles in Beijing."

I just nod. Luce is trying to be sweet. She is trying to impress me. It's been nine years, but I can tell she still has a crush on me. I find that I'm flattered.

But what really catches my eye is the familiar sign for ice cream cakes on a new building facade. "Carvel!" I cry. "I haven't been to one since I was a kid."

I can't believe it. A full store. Fancy, too. Awning, plate glass windows, neon sign.

I haven't tasted a Carvel cake since my brother's eighth birthday.

Luce's voice is too loud inside the Jeep. "Do you want to stop? It's the first Carvel in Beijing."

We stop. Luce pulls into an alley lined with cars haphazardly parked alongside the bricks of the hutong walls. She finds a spot and eases her Jeep into place as a few bicyclists whiz past angrily ringing their tinny bells.

"I'm impressed," I say, and I am. I can't imagine driving and parking in Beijing. I've been coming to China for nearly a decade, first as a language student and now for research for my dissertation, but taking public transportation is the extent of my courage. Maybe there's truth to the cliché about historians studying the past because we're not comfortable in the present.

The air is moist and thick at the height of summer, but at least there are trees on this particular street, charming somehow French-looking plane trees that are strung with colored lights. The Carvel is a fancy place here, belying its strip mall associations. There are freezers of frozen cakes, a bright counter, tables to sit at. There are some smart-looking young intellectuals with fancy eyeglasses and cool t-shirts, two young women with expensive purses. Six years after Tiananmen, I have to admit the city has certainly embraced the concept of moving on.

"So what would you like?" Luce asks brightly. She is being an exceptionally good sport.

I'm doing something cliché and touristy, and I know that Luce avoids these things in general. She wants to be the cool American in China, the almost-a-local-if-only-she-weren't-so-Caucasian-looking, not the tourist who goes to every Western franchise in Beijing, but she's doing it for me. The last time we'd been together had not ended well. She cheated on me with a student, and I on her with a man, but she's the one who feels guilty, and I'm the one who still feels aggrieved, and that's why she's willing to accompany me to this obscenely tacky place and politely ask me what I want to order.

The young woman behind the counter smiles prettily. Luce speaks to her in Mandarin, and the girl giggles and tells Luce how wonderful her Chinese is. For all Luce's efforts to become a local, she can't undo the privilege that comes from every imported American movie and TV show and their white stars. She's treated like a celebrity, like an exotic high-end consumer good here. This, too, used to be a sore point between us. I was jealous of the attention she received, and Luce resented my ability to pass as a local.

"I would like a slice of ice cream cake," I say deliberately in English.

"Very good," the girl says. "What flavor?"

And I know immediately, chocolate with mint chip. Jeremy's favorite.

I take the plate to the counter by the window, choose the corner seat. I don't want any distractions. It's been so long, and this is the last place I expected to find a remnant from the ashes of my childhood. I cut a corner with the edge of my fork.

The salty and the sweet.

Thick, heavy chocolate layer of crunch. Smooth layer of ice cream. Half-inch slab of icing over the whole thing.

I'M TEN-AND-A-HALF again, it's summer, and I'm plotting secrets with my mother. We always got a Carvel cake for my brother's birthday, personalized. The last one had a blue whale on top and "Happy Birthday, Jeremy!" in a bubble emerging from the whale's blowhole.

It was diabetes on a plate, but Jeremy had to have a Carvel cake or it wasn't special. It wasn't like a real birthday, he said.

We got him one every year, but we always pretended it was a surprise. Mom wouldn't mention it so Jeremy would think she forgot.

This time Mom took me along while Jeremy was playing at his best friend Seymour's house. "It's our secret," Mom said, and she winked at me.

I nodded, seriously.

Mom told Mrs. Beck we were going grocery shopping, or normally I would've stayed to play, too. The better for kickball teams. Seymour and Jeremy and one of the twins and me and the other twin. The little boys couldn't play so well yet, they would mostly run around and scream, and the teams were three against two, but it all evened out because I was an excellent kicker while Seymour had a lame leg. But today Mom said I couldn't stay. "Errands," she said, to throw off my brother.

So we were heading down the turnpike and I was talking about the exact cake we should get. Mint chocolate chip on top, chocolate on bottom, and the blue whale on top, because Jeremy was going through a phase and loved whales. Killers and beluga and baleen and even the underappreciated Norwegian sei whale. I knew exactly what the whale should look like, with one round eye and a slight smile on its blue face, like the one in the Richard Scarry book that first set Jeremy on the whale path.

Mom says, "Mmm-hmm, mm-hmm," like she wasn't really listening, and when I stopped talking, she didn't notice but continued squinting out the windshield, her lips pursed, like she was scanning the horizon for faraway things, not only trucks and cars. I was just happy to be included. Dad didn't plan secrets like this. He was busy with work, he was always busy. It was fun to go with Mom.

I DIDN'T plan on being the kind of person who likes secrets. What's charming in a child becomes something else in an adult. If I could find the words to explain this to Luce, I would apologize.

What I do instead, the moment we are back in the Jeep, is kiss her.

She's surprised, but she kisses me back. "I didn't expect this," she says.

I wish she would stop trying to talk. I hold onto her face with both hands and place my tongue in her mouth, and I can still taste the Carvel icing, FD&C Blue No. 1.

WHEN WE pulled up to the Carvel's that time with Mom, there was a man pacing in front. He was Caucasian and wearing a suit jacket but no tie. Standing on the sidewalk, looking at his watch, looking the wrong way, waiting.

Mom saw him and popped off her seat belt. "Wait here," she said in her serious voice, and slammed the door behind her. I was trapped because our Buick was still running, the keys in the ignition, and I couldn't just leave the car like that. Anything could happen.

I thought she was going to rush in to get Jeremy's cake and rush out again to me because of the man waiting there like that. I thought he was kind of creepy, and I thought she wanted me to wait in the car to protect me.

That's how I used to think in those days.

Mom went straight up to the man on the sidewalk and started talking to him, and he turned and smiled. Mom touched his arm and fiddled with her purse strap over her shoulder. The man touched her elbow, and she did not flinch. He kept his hand there, and then Mom nodded at the car with her chin, and the man looked at the car and saw me watching him through the windshield.

He smiled at me but stopped touching Mom's elbow.

I scowled at him.

He turned back to Mom, and they continued talking, I couldn't hear the words, just the texture. Mom's voice tumbling out, word after word, and then the man, a lower rumble, and suddenly a peal of Mom's laughter, the high notes puncturing the air.

I got a feeling in the pit of my stomach then, hard, like something was in there that wouldn't go down, and I could taste salt on the back of my tongue and something sweet, like I'd just eaten thick gooey icing, although I hadn't eaten since lunch, and that was a baloney sandwich with iceberg lettuce and yellow mustard on white bread, like normal, and then an apple and a chocolate chip cookie. And suddenly I thought, *It's the cookie.*

Flour and sugar and something oily were coating the top of my throat, the tops of my teeth. I tried to breathe through my mouth, but that only made it worse.

There were no bags in the car except my book bag, and I couldn't be sick in that.

I opened my door and flung myself toward the curb and threw up right there on the asphalt.

Both Mom and that man turned and saw me vomiting. Mom pursed her lips together sour plum style and hissed, "Jun-li, how could you?"

Back at home, Mom didn't speak to me again, she just put Jeremy's cake in the back of the freezer behind the Eggo waffles and the old half-gallon container of Neapolitan ice cream from the A&P and the boxes of Green Giant frozen vegetables. My brother wouldn't think to hunt around in the freezer. He wasn't like me. The month before Christmas I started hunting through the house to see where my mother might have hidden my presents. I volunteered to fold the laundry and put everything away just so I could check the linen closet, rummage through my father's sock drawer and my mother's underwear in her dresser. I checked under the bed and in the closets. But Mom always found a new place, one I hadn't thought of yet.

Jeremy, on the other hand, never thought to look for things. He was happy to play with his friends or his toy soldiers, lying on the floor of the family room on his belly, shooting *Pew! Pew! Pew!*, content to assume our parents would take care of his needs.

But my suspicious nature had a downside. I knew our parents argued in their bedroom. I was standing outside the door, quiet, the time Mom threw the clay statue we got on vacation at Wildwood against the wall and Dad smashed the blue bowl that held his cufflinks and tie tacks on the floor. After that, when I put away the laundry, I checked to make sure nothing was missing or broken: the empty Joy perfume bottle on Mom's dresser, the old cloisonné box from China that Ye-ye and Nai-nai had given them for their wedding, the knickknacks from the Circle Line Cruise we all took around the Statue of Liberty.

Now I knew about the man, too, but what about him I wasn't sure how to put into words.

LUCE AND I don't go to the hole in the wall place for noodles. We go back to Luce's apartment. She tells me first that she has a girl-friend, who is visiting her parents this weekend, but it's an "open relationship." Luce wants everything to be clear, so there will be no misunderstandings this time. I fight the urge to roll my eyes, but I get the impression that Luce is not calling the shots in this relationship. Maybe the girlfriend hasn't come out to her parents, I think. Maybe they're still hoping to set her up with a nice young man; maybe that's what this visit is all about and why Luce is the one who's acting vulnerable. She's blinking a lot, those long lashes fluttering over her troubled green eyes.

I nod like I'm listening, but what I'm doing is trying to forget. I want Luce to make me feel wanted, I want her body to distract me. I don't know what Luce wants. Maybe Luce wants to prove that she can still make me cry out, that I didn't really mean to leave her like that, that I should have forgiven her. I've been too distracted by my own wounds to think what kind I've left on Luce.

AFTERWARDS, ALL I can taste is the Carvel icing on the back of my tongue. Maybe it's the salt from her skin that throws the flavor into such sharp relief. I'd forgotten that the blue icing tastes like Play-Doh. Why had I ever liked it? But then I remember how I used to scrape the icing off. I only liked the chocolate parts. I was fussy like that as a child whereas Jeremy ate everything.

MOM HATED Carvel cakes.

The night of Jeremy's birthday, she refused to eat it. This was our private, just-family celebration before the real party that weekend when kids from school would come.

But that night Mom wasn't hungry. She pushed her plate away. "I just don't know how you can eat this," she said.

My father and brother looked up, startled, but she wasn't talking to them.

"My daughter, ha," she said. "My daughter likes this kind of thing." She picked up her fork between two fingers and let it dangle over the plate before dropping it in disgust. *Clank.*

I felt my nose burn. I forced my eyes to stare at the table, at the eight blue candles lying on the paper plate, the icing clinging to the ends, the blackened wicks, staring as though they were the most interesting candles in the world so that I wouldn't blink and start to cry.

"I have to go to class." Mom stood up, her chair scraping against the linoleum, *scrape scrape* against my ear.

I should have blurted it out then. I should have said her secret. But I didn't. Mom knew me too well.

Staring at the table top, I bit my tongue and felt a knot burning in my stomach, the acid rising. I'd barely make it to the tiny half bath off the kitchen before I threw up again.

I HAVE to go to the bathroom. Luce waits in bed, and I slip out from under the sheets and grab my clothes while I'm at it. I don't like walking around half-naked.

Luce has a Western style toilet, but the room is as small as a broom closet.

There is a retro-looking thermos for hot water, but it's empty and I'm not going to risk rinsing my mouth with water from the tap. I grab a tube of toothpaste and rub it across my teeth then spit and spit again, but now my mouth only tastes like Play-Doh and Aqua-fresh. I open the medicine cabinet, hoping to find some semblance of mouthwash, but there are only the usual assortment of prescriptions and ointments. Plus Playtex tampons placed strategically on the top shelf. Luce is very particular about what she puts into her body. Only those weird organic cotton ones that have no plastic applicator will do. I imagine the Playtex belong to the girlfriend, the one Luce thinks she's in an open relationship with. No matter what Luce may believe, the moment I see the tampons I know the woman is staking a claim.

The room is so small my knees nearly touch the wall in front of me when I sit on the toilet. I put my forehead in my hands, and all at once I am crying, hot thick tears pouring through my fingers, snot running down my face, a child's tears. I can't stop them.

It's the Play-Doh taste on my tongue.

AFTER JEREMY'S birthday that year, Mom announced that she was separating from our father. "I want you to know this situation has nothing to do with the two of you," she told us as we sat on the couch in the TV room, Jeremy's eyes wide and scared looking. "Your father and I love you very much," Mom said.

"I don't want you to go," he managed to blurt out, his eyes filling with liquid.

"It's because of Vincent, isn't it?" I sneered. I knew the man's name by then. I'd kept my ears open when my parents argued. I'd known to listen.

"Jun-li, don't make your brother upset," Mom said. She sat beside him on the sofa now, put her arms around him, and he hung his head into her lap and howled. She patted his back. "Look what you've done."

"Hush, hush," she rocked with Jeremy in her arms, like he was a baby and not an eight-year-old boy in a bowl cut and blue striped t-shirt.

I was jealous then. Jeremy was always the baby and I had to stand here watching my mother comfort him when I wanted to cry too. What I said was, "I hate you. You can go. You can go forever."

Mom looked up over Jeremy's back, her eyes narrowed at me, annoyed. "Jun-li, I need you to be reasonable. You're too old to act this way."

And I wanted to slap my brother then until his nose bled.

I stole all Jeremy's toy soldiers, the green plastic kind that came in a bag of twenty-five, and I threw them in the neighbor's trash. I grabbed his Fantastic Four comic collection and ripped them into shreds. I put salt in his guppy tank and glue on his Legos, but he didn't cry anymore, and Mom still left that summer.

I used to wish Dad had left and Mom had stayed. Even though I argued more with Mom and she was always angry at me. But Dad was always busy with work, he was always distracted, and he didn't worry about Jeremy the way Mom did, because Jeremy was her favorite.

At the very end of summer, Jeremy's best friend Seymour had a birthday party at the lake. He invited too many kids, his whole class, and because it was the last party before school started again, the whole class had shown up. It had been an especially hot and sticky week in late August, and most kids arrived with their little sisters and brothers in tow, parents figuring this was a good place to dump everyone for an afternoon, get them out of the sticky houses, let them blow off steam one last time.

The lake was artificial, not very large and not very clean. Normally Mom didn't let us swim there. Jeremy and I had both gotten ear infections the first summer we'd gone there for our swim lessons with the Red Cross when I was in second grade. After putting drops in our ears for a week, Mom was sick of it. She only ever took us to the pool at the Y after that, and then we stayed in the shallow end since we'd never finished the swim lessons.

Dad didn't know this, however. Or at least he didn't think about it. He let Mrs. Beck take us. Mrs. Beck was happy to have me along because she knew I was dependable. I'd heard her say this to Mom once, which meant she could leave the twins with me and go do other things and I'd have to take care of them.

No one was watching out for Jeremy after he and Seymour had a fight about who was cheating as they sat on the bank with their action figures, the Hulk versus the Thing, and Seymour threw sand into Jeremy's eyes. I could hear the argument from where I stood. Seymour was used to getting his way on account of his bum leg, Jeremy was kind in that way, but this time Jeremy got up and left.

Out of the corner of my eye I saw his chunky self run across the sand, but I didn't follow. I didn't intervene. I told myself I was too busy looking after the twins, who were tossing a beach ball on the edge of the water. In truth, I was angry at Jeremy for being our mother's favorite, and I let him go.

Mr. Tralucci was the one who noticed Jeremy had been gone for a while. He had some kind of father's sixth sense.

Then everyone had to get out of the water. Everyone stood in clumps on the artificial beach, on the dirt mixed with the imported sand, shivering, while the adults counted heads, and the lifeguards blew their whistles, and then some of the men shouted, and one of the lifeguards jumped into the water and swam to the wood dock on the other side of the lake, where they used to make us dive off during the Red Cross swim lessons.

They wouldn't let us kids see Jeremy's body.

A hole opened up in my guts then, and I crouched by the side of the lake, heaving.

After that, my parents did not get the divorce I'd been bracing for. Whatever differences might have driven them apart, Jeremy's drowning now brought them back together, locked in a kind of pain that was much, much worse.

AS A child, I blamed myself. I understood that I was a vengeful kind of person. I had wanted to hurt my mother. I had been angry at my brother. Who was to say I hadn't subconsciously willed this disaster?

There's a proverb in classical Chinese about digging two graves when you prepare to take revenge: for your enemy and yourself. In my case there was only one grave, reserved for the one truly innocent person in my life.

I MIGHT never have seen Luce again if mutual acquaintances had not put us in touch, letting me know that Luce had moved to Beijing.

Luce had apologized long ago. She said she was not good with endings. It was her fault, she said, taking up with her student while still sleeping with me. She had not meant to hurt me, she said.

And I thought I'd gotten over her, the rejection, the feeling that I was not good enough, the need to prove that she should never have let me get away, but no. I was apparently the Freudian cliché, intent upon repeating my history in an attempt at mastery, only to fail and fail again.

Thinking about my own pathetic behavior helps me to get a grip.

So I will myself to stop crying and I'm sitting on the toilet, realizing there is no paper, not to wipe my ass or blow my nose, when I hear the front door swing open.

Click clack. Someone's heels on the floor. Then *thud thud.* Someone kicking off her shoes. It has to be the girlfriend returning. I pull up my pants and look for a place to hide, but there is only me and the toilet. There is not enough room to squeeze behind the commode. I hold my breath as I hear the girlfriend padding across the apartment. She lets out a little squeal like a mouse in a trap as she finds Luce in bed. There is a creak of springs. She's apparently launched herself onto the bed.

"Hui lai le!" Luce exclaims theatrically, loud enough to wake the dead. *You're back!* She obviously is hoping I'll hear. I guess there's open and then there's not-this-open.

And I find myself thinking of all that I could do in this moment to royally screw Luce's life.

Revenge fantasy #1:

I could march dramatically into their bedroom and shout, "You lied to me! Shuo huang! Shuo huang!" I'd been crying so much, I might even be able to conjure up new tears.

Revenge fantasy #2:

I could march dramatically into their bedroom and shout, "What the fuck? Ni gan ma?"

Revenge Fantasy #3:

I could slam the bathroom door, scaring everyone, and stomp dramatically to the front door and slam that, too, leaving Luce to explain the mystery to her girlfriend.

Revenge Fantasy ∞:

I could imagine a million dramatic scenarios all to prove that I
was not the patsy or a pushover. On and on and on. Each one more
ridiculous than the last.

PERHAPS IF I had a therapist, I might discover my desire to be a
historian is tied to some deep misunderstanding of my own past,
some traumatic need to revisit what is long gone, to dredge it back
into the present for examination, for endless flagellation of those
actors long dead, second-guessing their motivations, trying to explain and make right decisions that are long past.

Perhaps what I really need is to embrace the Buddhism of my
grandparents and to live in the present. To breathe in, breathe out,
live in the moment. (Actually, I have no idea if this is the Buddhism
of my ancestors or simply the lite version that has filtered down
to my generation through Allen Ginsberg and the Beats and the
Counterculture, but never mind. That is a debate for another time.)

For example, if I am honest, I must admit that Luce's apartment
is not, in fact, all that nice. It was only nice in my mind because
Luce made it seem cool and trendy and desirable to live in an old
renovated hutong instead of a new building.

In fact my hotel is far more comfortable, and when I leave Beijing in a couple days, I'll be staying on the campus of Nanjing
University, this time in the so-called foreign experts' dormitories,
which are modern and well-appointed. I scoffed at such luxuries
when I was an undergrad, it had seemed inauthentic, but really, I
am tired of roughing it while doing research. It will be nice to have
a shower with hot water and air conditioning and a kitchen of my
own with electric appliances.

I know deep down that Jeremy's death was an accident.

Blaming myself is like blaming my mother. A way to keep the

pain alive, to relive it, and in some way keep Jeremy alive, never moving on.

In the present, I think about my options, revenge and otherwise. I think of all the awkward things that would have to be said. I think of the potential for anger and blame. I think of the people I have hurt in my own life.

I realize I do not need to see what Luce's new girlfriend looks like. I already know. Someone who glows brighter in Luce's gaze than she ever has on her own.

I find I can accept this.

I SLIP out of the bathroom, tiptoeing down the hall, crouching my way past the bedroom door as though that will make me less visible.

My shoes are still by the front door, but behind Luce's backpack, where she'd dropped it in a moment of passion. I find my purse under the coat rack.

Then I slip out the door.

I'm not trying to make trouble for Luce and the new girlfriend.

THERE IS a break in the smog today, and the sunshine is bright enough to make me squint.

Fashionable young couples stroll by arm in arm. A taxi beeps its way through pedestrians trying to cross the street. A billboard advertising shampoo flashes a Russian model's face. I can see the golden arches just ahead, a KFC at the corner, a Starbucks, a Pizza Hut. A shop window is plastered with posters for Motorola. A colorful umbrella over a pushcart advertises Coca-Cola.

In the shade of some plane trees, an old man has set up a make-shift fruit stand with piles of orange persimmons spread across a striped tarpaulin. I can imagine a time when there will no longer be old men selling persimmons on the street, when such old-fashioned treats will be a memory, and everyone will buy fruit waxed and displayed in identical mounds in an air-conditioned store.

I buy a *jin* of persimmons from the old man. He measures them on an old-style hand weight, putting the fruit in a metal tray on a pulley attached by wire to a metal bar with the weights marked on it. I hand him my crumpled bills, and he grabs a sheet of newspaper from the pile at his feet, rolls it into a cone and dumps my persimmons inside.

Walking down the sidewalk, I pluck out a largish persimmon, pull at the skin and bite inside. The pulp and juice explode over my tongue, the sweetness coating every inch of my mouth, erasing that cloying blue icing taste, as well as the salt of Luce's flesh and the briny flavor leftover from my snot and tears. I hunch over the persimmon melting in my hands, devouring its flesh until there's nothing left but the skin, which I toss in the gutter and then start on another. I slip off the skin, and eat and eat, suck and chew and swallow, and bite again, again, again, savoring each drop of flesh, as though I'll never be sated, as though I can make this moment last forever.

SHOUTING MEANS I LOVE YOU

HURRY UP." MY father knocked on the bathroom door. "We don't want to keep the General waiting."

"There's plenty of time." I glanced at my watch. "More than three hours."

"All that traffic! We can't be late!" he shouted into the crack of the door. "Ye-ye told me, 'Never forget what General Shih has done for the family.'"

"I'm going to the bathroom! Go away!" I said. I was temporarily a teenager again, and my father was his old prickly self. We'd once shouted at each other for more than three and a half hours straight. My mother had cried, my brother had cried, and still we'd continued shouting.

Now he was eighty and a widower, and it had been a long time since the fights of my adolescence. In recent years, my father had grown anxious. Everything scared him. The ongoing wars, the economy, the competition for schools. "I was lucky. I had it easy," he'd said on the drive to San Francisco from the airport, the man who survived the Sino-Japanese War as a child. "What about the kids?" He meant my brother's children. "I'm too old, I won't live to see it, I'm going to die soon, but global warming, what will happen?"

My stomach had knotted. Was it a plea for attention? Did he want me to reassure him that he was not old, he would live, he was not dying soon? Did he want me to deny climate change? I didn't know how to console him.

Now as I hurried to change my clothes in the bathroom and fix my make-up, I could hear my father fussing in my bedroom, opening the closet, rummaging for something. I wanted to ask him what he was looking for, but I also wanted to avoid an argument. I bit my tongue and rummaged in my make-up case for my eyeliner.

But once we were on the highway, driving to the General's house in the South Bay, my father was in high spirits.

"Ye-ye told me General Shih is the most important person in our lives. You must never forget him. He saved our family. He got us the passports. Not everyone was allowed to have passports in those days in Taiwan. But he got them for us and we could come to America."

"I thought you were already in America by the time everyone else needed the passports. You came first. To Ohio."

"What?" my father said. "What are you mumbling about?"

My father was mostly deaf, but he wouldn't get a hearing aid. I took him to an audiologist, 70 percent loss in both ears, but he refused. A hearing aid was the end, in his mind. He remembered Ye-ye's hearing aid in the 1970s. The coiled plastic cord that ran from the box hanging outside his ear to the battery in his shirt pocket, like he had a phone permanently attached to his ear. First Ye-ye got the hearing aid, then Nai-nai died, then overnight Ye-ye was old, then he was dead. That was how my father remembered it.

Perhaps it was a good sign that he didn't want the hearing aid. It was his final act of defiance against the encroachment of age. He'd had the heart surgery, the stent, the radiation for his prostrate. He gave up red meat, eggs, his beloved *rou sung*, because the desiccated pork was all cholesterol and salt and MSG. He'd gotten his cataracts removed one after the other, wearing first a left eye patch then a right. He resisted the cane for a long time, but then he fell last winter walking to the mailbox and had to crawl the length of his driveway to get back inside his house. That scared him. So he had two canes now, an indoor one and an outdoor one. He checked the rubber tips assiduously for wear.

"When's the last time you saw him?" I asked.

"What?"

"WHEN'S THE LAST TIME YOU SAW THE GENERAL?" I repeated.

"I don't know. Years ago. When did we come here?"

"You came in 1952. Ye-ye, Nai-nai, Uncle Truman, and Uncle Dwight came in fifty-five."

"I think I saw him that time in Hawaii. When was that? Ye-ye was still alive."

"Maybe 1980?"

"I don't know. A long time ago."

My father fell silent, then dozed off. He had stayed up late last night preparing his gifts, wrapping them carefully, each gift in its respective bag. Then he'd seen my Barneys New York bag, the sleek black paper with the elegant white lettering and the thick straps, the one I'd gotten with my splurge purchase last sales season. I'd hid it in my closet before he came, but my father had found it somehow. He had a sixth sense for bags.

Now it held the mochi and the General's book (each in their separate paper bags within).

As we emerged from the Bay Bridge into the intense sunshine onto the I-880 exchange, my Honda's tires thumped over potholes or speed grading or god knows what else wrong with the infrastructure today. I thought the vibrations would wake my father, but he only shifted a little, his sleep undisturbed.

He fell asleep easily during the day, basically whenever he was seated, in front of the television blaring the cable news, in the armchair with his copy of *World Journal* still open and clenched in both his hands.

At night he couldn't sleep at all. Had to take pills. First it was Ambien until the grandkids discovered him sleepwalking, wandering the house with his eyes wide open. He had no idea who they were, and it had scared them. Now it was lorazepam.

But last night they hadn't worked. He'd woken me in the middle of the night.

"I can't sleep," he said.

"You're excited about tomorrow," I said from under my sleeping bag. My apartment was too small for a guest bed or a sofa or any of those suburban amenities. When my father visited, I gave him the bed and slept on the floor.

Then he turned on the overhead light and rooted through his luggage. He turned on the kitchen light and opened some drawers.

"What are you looking for?" I sat up on the floor.

"Don't worry, I won't get addicted," he said. "I cut the pills in half."

But now in the car I worried that he'd taken too much. He was snoring, his chin in his chest. I remembered how my mother used to exclaim about his ability to sleep head forward. She needed to sleep head back. I hadn't thought about these differences in a long time.

As we approached the exit to Milpitas, Siri ordered, "Turn Right! Turn Right!" and my father awoke, shaking his head.

"Are we late?"

"A little," I admitted.

The General's home was on a circular drive, small houses with green lawns and lovely trellises of pink bougainvillea.

"These are million-dollar homes now," my father sighed. "After teaching for fifty years, I still can't afford to live here."

There was a time shortly after the turn of the new millennium I used to dream there'd be a second dot-com bust and I'd be able to afford a bigger apartment. No more.

"You wouldn't be able to get a house like yours here," I said, trying to console him. In Ohio, he had 3500 square feet, a finished basement, a yard with trees. My parents had bought the house after I'd left for college. I'd never lived in their "dream house." Now my father complained about the winters, the snow, the hot summers, the tornadoes, the cost of repairing the roof.

"My house is too old," he said. "The plumber says I need a new water heater. That's ten thousand dollars. And the shingles need repairing. The gutters are one big mess. One more winter like last winter and I'm finished."

"Okay, here we are." I eased past the recycling and trash bins on the curb and pulled into the narrow driveway.

"Yep, this is the life," my father said, gazing at the tiny, manicured lawn, the blooming rose bush before the front steps. "Too bad your apartment is too small. I can't even move in with you."

He left his cane in the front seat.

"Don't you want that?"

"Leave it!" he hissed. "Where's the bag?"

I popped the trunk and pulled out my lovely Barneys bag.

My father snatched it from my hands. "Let's go. We're late."

I grabbed him under the elbow and helped him walk up the drive. "Are you sure you don't want your cane?"

"I'm going to be sitting," he said with dignity.

At the base of the steep brick steps, he handed me the Barneys bag and gripped the metal banister tightly then pulled himself up one step at a time. I hovered in case he fell back. At the top, he held out his hand, and I gave him back the Barneys bag. He nodded like royalty acknowledging a page.

"Ring the doorbell," he said.

I tried the bell by the door, but I didn't hear it ring. I could hear a television blaring inside, it sounded like a football game.

I tried the bell again.

"Maybe you'd better knock."

I knocked. I could still hear the football game.

I pulled out my phone and looked up the number. I could hear the phone ringing inside the house. Finally someone picked up. "Wei?" said a woman's voice. I handed the phone to my father.

"We're here!" he shouted in Mandarin. "We're here!"

"Where are you?"

"Outside your house! Open the door!"

"Where are you? Who is this?"

I was afraid she might hang up, so I tried knocking on the front door.

I could hear shuffling inside. Then the door opened. A very tall, very elderly man peered at us through the screen. He was dressed exactly like my father: khaki chinos held up by a brown leather belt, sweater vest, cotton oxford collar shirt, and golf cap. "General Shih!" my father proclaimed.

"Professor!" The General beamed.

The General ushered us inside. His living room was small but tastefully decorated with scrolls of calligraphy on the walls, doilies with hand tatting on the sagging sofa and over-stuffed armchairs, various cloisonné vases, and a giant flat-screen TV blaring on the far wall. It looked almost exactly like my father's living room in Ohio.

My father presented his gifts, opening the bag with the book in it for the General.

"This is exactly the book I've been wanting to read," the General said.

Then he handed the bag of mochi to the General's wife who grabbed it and took it into the kitchen.

"Please sit," said the General. "Would you like some tea?"

The General hurried after his wife then returned carrying a metal try with two delicate looking teacups on saucers.

"You can walk pretty good!" my father said.

"My wife is the sick one," the General said. "She just got out of the hospital."

"He put me there," the wife said.

"Careful, they are hot," the General said, placing a teacup on the end table near my father's elbow.

"You're too kind," my father said. "My father told me, 'Never forget the General. He is the most important person in our lives. He saved our family.'"

"No, no, no," the General said.

"My father told me if not for you, the rest of the family would not have been able to come to America. You really helped them. You helped a lot of people."

"Your father was my teacher. He was a very good teacher."

My father and the General traded compliments like this back and forth, back and forth, and then the General's wife announced, "It's going to be too late to eat!"

"I've made a reservation," said the General. And for the first time, his eyes gleamed. He turned to me and said in slow, careful English, "Do you like Chinese food?"

"Yes," I said, wondering, did I look like someone who didn't?

"You're very lucky," my father said. "All these good restaurants! Where I live, we can't get good Chinese food."

"I know the best restaurant," he said, leaning forward almost conspiratorially. "As good as Hong Kong!"

"It's late!" his wife announced.

"Are you going to invite your son? Invite your son! We can all go in my daughter's car. She can drive us."

"My son," the General said. "He's probably working."

"Go ahead and call him."

The General bounded up the steps to his kitchen two at a time.

My father called after him, "You can walk pretty good! At my age, I can barely walk at all."

The wife paced in the foyer. She looked up when she heard the General call into the receiver, "Wei? Are you there?"

Before long, the General returned, shaking his head. "He can't come. He has work."

"Ah," my father said. "He's busy."

The General's wife blew air over her teeth.

My father refused to let me help him get out of the chair, and then he teetered across the floor. The General took hold of his arm and helped him to the door.

"You're lucky! You don't need a cane!" my father said. "I fell a few years ago. Slipped on the ice. I could have died. A colleague of mine, a young woman, she moved from UCLA. She went outside to smoke one night and fell. They found her the next morning. Frozen solid. Dead like that."

"It's that cold?" the General said, eyes wide.

"My daughter wants me to move in with her, she thinks it's too dangerous for me to spend the winter alone in my house, but her apartment is too small."

"Your daughter worries about you. She's a good daughter."

"She's a teacher. Teachers don't make any money. I taught fifty years and I can't afford to retire where I want. I have to live in that terrible cold place."

"Be careful!"

They were gingerly taking the front steps together, then shuffling to my car. I opened the doors and waited for them to climb inside, my father and the General in the back, his wife in the front passenger side seat.

"Where are we going? I can program it into my GPS," I said.

"She can tell you the directions," the General said in his careful English.

"Wang qian zou," his wife said, waving a hand down the street like a practiced traffic cop.

I followed her directions over to the Ranch 99 shopping center. The parking lot was packed, cars circling like land sharks, but I lucked out, a spot in front of a hair salon, just a video store, eyeglass emporium, and jewelry store down from the restaurant.

My father felt confident enough not to use his cane.

"I don't need it," he said after I held it out to him, frowning as though he'd never seen it before, as though I'd found some stranger's cane and now waved it at him, foolishly imagining it was his.

As the General and his wife walked to the restaurant, my father grabbed my arm tightly, and I could feel his body tremble and sway with each step.

Inside the Mayflower, the General rubbed his hands as he surveyed the carts wending their way around the crowded tables. "What do you like to eat?" he asked.

"You're lucky you can still eat! At my age, I don't know what I can eat. Ask my daughter."

"What does your father like to eat?" he asked me.

"Bland foods. No spice. No pork. Good for the heart."

The General's bushy white eyebrows fell.

"Don't eat what I can eat. Go ahead. Get what you like," my father said. "My daughter can eat."

Actually, that wasn't true either, I had enough food intolerances to catalog, but the General seemed heartened and began waving at the cart ladies: fried taro cakes, *shiu mai* dumplings, *xiao long* soup dumplings, giant mushrooms stuffed with pork, eggplant stuffed with shrimp, a tureen of fish soup, a clay pot of something that looked like fungus and tentacles, steamed barbecue pork buns, chicken feet, and small bowls of fried rice.

"That's too much," the General's wife said, scowling.

"Eat, eat!" the General said, spinning the lazy Susan towards my father. He stretched his chopsticks to pluck the fattest foods for my father.

"Really, I can't have that," my father protested.

"I know what he can eat," I said, and plunked some mushrooms onto my father's plate. "Don't eat the pork," I said in English.

"Eat eat!" the General said. "This is the best restaurant I have found. Authentic flavor."

"Don't be polite," my father said. "You should eat."

"He's not polite," the General's wife said. "Everyone says my husband is so polite, has the best manners, he's such a great man, but really he is terrible."

My father laughed politely.

"My husband is a scoundrel," she said. "Really he's the worst person on earth."

A waiter in a red coat walked by carrying a tray of porcelain teapots. "Here, here!" the General called. "Do you like black, oolong, jasmine, chrysanthemum tea?"

"He put me in the hospital for three months. He told them I was crazy," the General's wife said. "My own son wouldn't help me. He took all my money and gave it away. I don't have anything!"

"Your husband is a good man—" my father began.

"No, he's not!" she shrieked. "He's the worst man on earth! Everyone thinks my husband is a good man. But he is a bad man. God will judge him." She pulled a necklace with a cross pendant out from underneath her sweater. "I believe in God. I believe in heaven. My husband is a bad man!"

"Have some tea?" the General said, pouring the hot liquid into the tiny porcelain cup.

"Have something to eat," my father said, turning the lazy Susan, sending the mushrooms toward the General's wife.

She ignored the mushrooms but grabbed a bun and two chicken feet with her chopsticks.

I took up the teapot and filled her cup.

"So how is your new book coming along?" the General asked my father.

"My husband is such a bad man. He had all those women in all those places," she waved a chicken foot in the air for emphasis. "A bad man!"

She was so angry, her face changed color, darkening purplish along her jaw. Her black eyes flashed and the penciled lines of her eyebrows met. She gnashed the bones between her teeth.

I had no idea if anything she said about the General was rooted in truth or if perhaps she really was mentally ill or in some form of dementia, the past literally haunting her present, but it was clear in any case that she was very angry at her husband.

After we'd all pretended to eat, pushing everything around our plates, the General's wife had everything boxed to go and the General flagged the waiter and grabbed the bill.

"Let me pay!" my father said. "You have done so much for my family. My father said I must never forget how you have helped us."

"No," the General told my father. "Your father was my teacher. He was a very good teacher. I am inviting you and your daughter today."

I leaned close to my father's ear. "I can grab it from him," I said. "Should I?"

"No, no, no!" my father whispered back. "Let him. He wants to invite us."

I never understood the check ritual, when it was all right to let someone else pay, when I was supposed to play the filial daughter and snatch it from one of my father's colleague's hands so that we could pay instead. I shrugged and let the General pay the bill.

Then the General turned to his wife and held out his hand, and she rummaged in her purse for her wallet, took out a credit card, and handed it to him.

Walking back to the car, my father held onto the General's arm, and his wife leaned in toward me. "I remember the General telling me about your grandparents. He talked about them all the time," she said, a shrewd look on her face. "He said they argued all the time. He said he'd never seen anyone argue like that. The way they would shout!" Her lips thinned against her teeth in a half smile.

I looked her in the eye. "I know," I said. "It's how they communicated. Shouting for that generation practically meant 'I love you.'"

She looked startled. She must have imagined that I'd try arguing with her, and she was gearing up for a fight, but I wasn't going to take her bait. I didn't care what she thought. The General's wife turned away for a second, frowning.

"You aren't married," she said, as though she'd just realized this fact. "It's better not to be married. I should never have married. A happy life to be single."

Then the General and my father returned, and we walked back to the car talking of nothing more than the pleasant weather in Northern California in December, the tall palms silhouetted against the clear blue sky.

DRIVING BACK to San Francisco, I figured there would be less traffic on 101 than 880. Better than trying to cross the Bay Bridge on a Saturday afternoon at least. And for once, my traffic instincts paid off. We made it through 237 to 101 in twenty minutes, and then we were heading up the Peninsula, the oddly retro billboards for Silicon Valley's companies dotting the sides of the highway.

"The General's pretty lucky. He's older than me and didn't need a cane," my father said. "All those steps in his house! That would kill me!"

"It's ironic. Perfect health but a long, miserable marriage. The General's wife told me it was good not to be married."

"She said that?"

"She told me Ye-ye and Nai-nai argued and shouted all the time."

"Well." My father shook his head.

We drove along in silence for a while. I hesitated to put on NPR, thinking my father might need to fall asleep again, but he remained fully awake, staring out the windshield, unblinking.

"I worry about your brother," my father said at last. "I don't worry about you, I know you'll be all right, but I worry about him."

"Don't say that." That's what my mother used to say before she went through the house and took all my "extra" things, clothes, shoes, toys, and sent them to her sisters' kids. "I don't worry about you, you'll be all right," was code for this-is-why-I'm-going-to-take-your-stuff. I learned early to hide things I liked: books under the mattress or slid between the bed and the wall, favorite dolls hidden in old shoeboxes pushed to the back of my closet.

"He quit his job," my father said. "He gave up his good job like that."

"He wanted to start his own company."

"Who gives up tenure?"

"He does." I sighed. "It's the era of entrepreneurship."

"You could tell him—"

"He won't listen to me. I'm not going to get involved in this." My mother was good with messages. Tell your brother this, she'd say. Tell your father to do such and such. Now that she was gone, my father had picked up her habit. But I wasn't going to fall into that old trap again. Years of therapy had helped me to see the light. "If you have something to say, you'll have to tell him yourself," I said.

My father stared out the windshield without replying.

"So what happened to the General's wife?" I wanted to change the subject.

"To think, they've been married all this time," my father said. "More than sixty years."

"Did you ever meet her before? In Taiwan?"

My father shook his head, trying to remember. "Maybe in Hawaii. I think she was a real beauty when she was young."

"Was she this unhappy then?"

"I don't know. I don't remember noticing anything."

"No wonder the son didn't want to come. What a nightmare."

"I was so lucky," my father said. "Mama was so nice to me. I was a lucky man."

And then he sniffed because thinking of my mother still made my father want to cry.

I thought he might break down, in fact, and dug in the space between the seats for the box of Kleenex I used to keep there, but it must have slid into the back. My fingers touched coins, a pen, what felt like a sock, an old plastic bag, but I couldn't find the tissues.

"I forgive you," my father said, breaking the silence.

"What?"

"The General's wife is so bitter. She should just forgive him. They're too old. What's the point? That's what I think at my age." He nodded and settled back into the seat, satisfied. "I just want you to know," my father said, "I forgive you."

"For what?" I said.

"For everything."

It was just unbelievable. I had taken care of my mother when she was ill. I had taken care of my father after his heart surgery. Had they paid me? Had they worried that this might be a hardship for me? Had they asked my brother to take time off the tenure track to help them? And now, here it was my winter break, I had friends going on trips, Hong Kong, Myanmar, but no, I'd told them all I couldn't go because my father had said he wanted to visit me. So I let him come and gave him my bed, and I drive him across the Bay to visit his crazy old friends and play the filial game, and now this! When I was a teenager, he'd spent money on my brother for a car, a motorcycle, a three-wheeler even, and I wasn't allowed to go out after dark, and the housework I'd done, and the cooking, and who had to work her way through college? I felt the old familiar anger settling into my stomach again, and I remembered why I'd wanted to move far away from my family in the first place, vowing to stay away.

I took a deep cleansing breath, the kind the therapist recommended when she talked about family dynamics and repeating the cycle and breaking the cycle, and I exhaled slowly over my teeth. I tried to count to ten but only made it to five.

"I forgive you, too," I said tightly.

"You're welcome," my father agreed.

"No, I said I FORGIVE YOU. I didn't thank you."

"You don't need to thank me," my father said. "I'm your father."

"You're not listening to me!"

"Why are you shouting?"

"Because you can't hear me!"

"Why are you shouting?"

"OH, my god," I said, clenching and unclenching the wheel. And I was fifteen years old all over again, arguing at the dinner table: "You don't listen to me!" I was twelve, I was eight. My father was lecturing me instead of answering a question, speaking as though to a room filled with undergraduates diligently taking notes.

I took another even deeper breath and exhaled.

"I'm sorry," I said.

"Why are you sorry?"

"You said you forgive me. So, I say I'm sorry."

"What for? What happened?"

"Good lord. This is going to kill me."

"What's going to kill you? What's the matter with you?"

"How come you can hear me now? Half the time you can't hear anything I say!"

"Don't be angry when you drive," my father said. "You shouldn't —Watch! Watch!" He pointed out the window at a giant white bus switching into our lane.

I hit my brakes just in time to prevent being sideswiped. "Goddamn Google bus!" I pounded my wheel.

HONK! HONK!

"Oh, that's the Google bus!" my father said. He pushed his glasses higher up onto his nose. "That's what it looks like."

"Look out your window," I said. "I'll pass them so you can see. The techies are all trying to hide inside, but we all know what they look like."

I sped up so that my father could watch the white side of the bus rush by his window. The bus's windows were tinted, but I could imagine the smooth-faced tech workers within serenely checking the price of their stock options on their laptops. I honked again as we passed.

HONK! HONK! HONK!

The third honk felt especially satisfying.

"It doesn't look like anything special," my father said. "I'm not impressed."

"Neither am I."

"You're my daughter," he said. "We're not impressive."

"No. *Impressionable*, not impressive."

"Yes. We're the same, you and me."

I didn't even try to take the third cleansing breath. All that deep breathing only made me feel light-headed anyway. I gripped the wheel and kept my eyes on the road, and I thought, *Why not?* We were the same, in our way. Same blood, same family, same method of communicating, therapy be damned.

Eventually, my father fell asleep, his chin on his chest.

And we didn't argue again, not for the entire drive back to San Francisco.

ACKNOWLEDGMENTS

Many thanks to my friends and family for all their encouragement during the writing of these stories, especially Kate Agathon, Nerissa Balce, Penelope Dane, Nina de Gramont, Carolyn Desalu, Sheryl D. Fairchild, Jeni Fong, Gwynn Gacosta, David Gessner, Gary Kramer, Sue Jean Halvorsen, Felicia Luna Lemus, George Lew, Beth Roddy, Lorraine Saulino-Klein, Nitasha Sharma, Frances Kai-Hwa Wang, Nina Wolff, Howard Wong, Yi-Li Wu, and Susan Xin Xu; many thanks to my former students and colleagues in the Creative Writing Department at the University of North Carolina Wilmington, where many of these stories were written—the creative atmosphere and sense of camaraderie that you all fostered inspired me greatly; special thanks to my colleagues at San Francisco State University for their support and good will; and very special thanks to my father, Winberg Chai, for his love and constant enthusiasm.

I would like to thank the editors of the journals who first published some of these stories in somewhat different form, including Elizabeth Weld at *The Grist: A Journal of the Literary Arts*; Jon Tribble at *Crab Orchard Review*; Trish O'Hare, publisher, at GemmaMedia Open Door; Allison Grimaldi-Donahue at *Queen Mob's Tea House*; and Susan Burmeister-Brown and Linda Swanson-Davies at *Glimmer Train*. I am honored that the *Crab Orchard Review* awarded the Jack Dyer Prize in Fiction to my story "Fish Boy."

I am grateful to the team at Blair—my editor, Robin Miura; publisher, Lynn York; and cover designer, Laura Williams—for taking such good care of this manuscript at every step of the publication process. It has been a pleasure to work with you all. And very special thanks to Tayari Jones, whose own work has been such an inspiration over the years, for choosing this collection as the winner of the Bakwin Award for Writing by a Woman.